THE
BLUE LIGHT
SPECIAL

An Arresting Collection
of Humorous Police Stories

By Leo Mudd

ISBN: 1450547133
ISBN-13: 9781450547130

ACKNOWLEDGMENTS

If I could take a moment of your time: You have a book inside you waiting to be shared with others to make their lives fuller. I want to say thanks to those of you who shared that speck of a moment of your life with us.

A great big thanks to Byron Crawford for his encouragement to put this book together and his foundation story in The Courier-Journal that received great response. Also to Jack Hicks of the Kentucky Post who also contributed to that foundation.

A truck-load of thanks to Dr. Ann Weeks who guided the plan for this great trip of humor.

Thanks to my family – Joyce, my wife, and Kevin, LaTina and Chris, my children, who always say, "Dad, you can do it."

Finally, a thank-you to all the folks with relatives who have paid that great sacrifice so the world we share could be a little safer to laugh in.

This book is dedicated to our fallen comrades who never got to print their stories.

Leo Mudd

*To all those
who have served.*

FOREWORD

BY GEORGE THOMPSON

As one who has spent the last 16 years traveling across the country and around the world teaching peace officers the tactical art of Verbal Judo, I have been continually amazed at how "healthy" officers are in this most difficult of professions. I give much of the credit to the quality of their HUMOR.

Humor, as depicted in Leo Mudd's marvelous book, binds our fraternity together as it does in no other profession. Over the years, much has been made of the "gallows humor" of the officer, a humor which allows him or her to get through the most brutal scenes of human carnage and human tragedy. Humor can give us a saving perspective to complete our work where others would just collapse in emotional reaction.

But many of these stories written and collected by former Kentucky State Trooper Leo Mudd also suggest another dimension to police humor – our basic humanity. Civilians will get a peek behind the Blue Wall. They will see themselves in the officer, and, perhaps, they will see we are truly part of the greater society we serve. They will see wonderful examples of human blunders, rank stupidity, amazing goodness, and, yes, even a tenderness for the people we serve. Officers come across in these pages as warm human beings, capable of so much caring and having a desire to do the job correctly, yet marvelously flawed — just like all of us! Perhaps in reading these true stories, parables of every officer, really, people can feel closer to the cop on the street, can see him as more than just a uniform or a badge.

Every officer has his or her stories to tell, and this unique book is dedicated to our fallen comrades who never had time to tell their full complement of stories. This collection speaks for them, too.

For me, once a full-time officer and now a commissioned reserve officer, these stories just make me feel better! The spider monkey story, for example, makes me feel better about once locking the keys in my vehicle as I went to arrest a violent man with a knife. On returning to my car, I pushed the man up against it, said, "Get in!" and wrenched the door – nothing happened! There I stood waiting for a backup unit with a tool to unlock the car, while making it appear to the growing crowd that he couldn't get in the car until he stopped yelling and struggling. The officer who arrived immediately sensed my real problem and unlocked the door with the tool hidden from the crowd. Thanks for covering for me!

We have all been there, been in these stories somehow, and these parables strengthen our fraternity, and connect us to our fellow human beings. For all those readers who have heard cops say, "Police work is the greatest job in the world," this book will tell you why. God, police work is FUN! Enjoy what Leo Mudd has assembled for you!

George Thompson, a former police officer and currently a reserve officer, is founder and president of the Verbal Judo Institute in Albuquerque, N.M.

INTRODUCTION

BY BYRON CRAWFORD

My first encounter with Trooper Leo Mudd was in the glow of flickering blue lights through the window of the WHAS-TV News cruiser that my cameraman and I drove. He was asking to see an operator's license for the speeding ticket he would hand back through the window.

I didn't see Trooper Mudd for a few years after that. Then one summer I crossed paths with him again, on the stage of the Official Kentucky State Championship Old-Time Fiddlers Contest at Rough River, where we were co-emcees of the event, along with our old friend, the late Jodie Hall.

In the years that followed, I would come to appreciate Leo for his compassion for others, his dedication to duty, his creativity and talent, and for his wonderful sense of humor – which I had not seen when he and I met through the car window.

Now, I know Leo Mudd as the creator of a cartoon character, called "Wuz," that for several years was a regular feature of Kentucky's most widely circulated publication, "Kentucky Living" magazine. He invented and marketed his own candy bar. And he has touched thousands of young people with his anti-drug programs in schools around the country, and he now teaches the art of Verbal Judo.

As we got to know each other as friends, Leo often shared with me many of the comical predicaments that he and his fellow law enforcement officers experienced on their jobs. So hilarious were some of the stories that I urged Leo – right from the start – to save them and compile them in a book one day.

In "The Blue Light Special," Leo and a host of other law enforcement officers have lifted their badges and shown us their hearts. They have invited us to laugh with them at their silly blunders, and to witness some of the ridiculous situations in which they find themselves.

We like the sound of their laughter. And to our surprise, their smiles, when reflected in blue light, really do make the blue lights special.

Byron Crawford is a columnist for The Courier-Journal in Louisville, Ky., and host of "Kentucky Living" on KET (Kentucky Educational Television).

BLUE LIGHT SPECIAL

The day I graduated from the Kentucky State Police Academy was one of the happiest days of my life! I can remember standing there in that perfectly ironed uniform thinking I couldn't wait to drive my marked Kentucky State Police cruiser right on home and park it in my driveway. I immediately asked my sergeant where my cruiser was and if I could go get it. We were standing in the Capitol Building in Frankfort, Ky., and he said my cruiser was parked outside, and, yes, I could get it.

I ran so fast down those steps to where it was parked. When my eyes caught sight of that cruiser, I couldn't help but think that it looked a bit like Deputy Barney Fife's car on "The Andy Griffith Show."

It looked like that to me because of the six-foot-long antenna coming off the side of the left fender. Those antennas were so long that when you sped down the highway in pursuit of a violator, you had to be careful stepping out of the cruiser or that antenna might just come flying back and swat you in the back of the head! Remember the antenna.

On the top, right in the middle of the cab, was my blue light. We called it a bubble gum machine because it looked like a bubble gum machine. Remember the blue light.

Inside the cruiser, I didn't have a protective screen between the front and back seats. Remember that too.

Now that you know what my cruiser looked like, let me tell you about the first drunk I arrested. I chased the man down, stopped him, arrested him and placed him in the back seat of that old cruiser. I felt proud. I had made my first arrest all by myself! I proceeded to the jail with the man in custody.

Suddenly I felt that old drunk's hands come slithering up around my neck. As I pulled to the side of the road, he nearly pulled me right back over the seat. I felt something wet and slimy in my ear. It was that old drunk's lips. Then I heard him scream, "You gonna kill my monkey!"

Adrenaline put me over the top and into the back seat with him. I looked at him and shouted, "What do you mean, I'm going to kill your monkey?"

That old drunk answered, "You rolled my windows up. You locked my doors. It's a hundred degrees out there. You left my pet spider monkey in the back seat of my car. You're going to fry my monkey!"

I looked at him and thought for a moment. I thought he was a clever con artist. Then, I thought again – what if he does have a monkey and it does fry? I could see the next day's headlines in my mind: Trooper fries pet monkey.

I calmed the man down and headed back to his car. I found a cute little spider monkey sitting in the back seat, rocking back and forth, sweat rolling down between its eyes. That little monkey must have thought he was in a microwave oven.

The monkey had a collar with an eight-foot leash. I knew I had to rescue the creature and somehow get him to my cruiser without any passing motorists catching sight of a uniformed Kentucky state trooper walking back to his car being pulled along by a monkey on a leash.

As I walked to my cruiser, I could see the old drunk had crawled into the driver's seat and was chatting with his sloppy lips drooling all over my police radio. I just knew he was talking to my boss about how I had fried his monkey.

I had to make a quick decision because I remembered I had left my keys in the ignition. At that moment, I reached up and grabbed the tip end of that long antenna, bent it over toward the back of the cruiser, put the ring at the end of the monkey's leash around the antenna, slid it on down and secured the little creature.

I ran to the driver's door, pulled the drunk out and placed him in the back seat again. As I shut the door, I heard my police radio calling me to an accident in my county. I was the only officer on patrol, so I needed to go quickly. Not being used to making so many fast decisions, I did exactly what they told me to do. I slid into the driver's seat, put on my safety belt, fired that big engine up and went speeding down the road at 90 mph.

Well, about two miles down the road, I noticed that old drunk crying and slobbering again in the back seat. He was looking out the back window and making all kinds of noise. He slapped me on the shoulder and said, "You don't have to stop now. You already killed my monkey."

As soon as I heard that, I remembered where I had put the monkey. I pulled over to the side of the road, rested my head on the steering wheel and said a little prayer that went like this: "God, if you ever made a monkey that could run 90 mph, please let it be this one."

I jumped out of my cruiser. I ran down the road. I looked in the surrounding fields. I searched the ditches. No monkey. All at once, I remembered that the accident I was headed to was more important than that monkey. I figured he was in Monkey Heaven.

I bowed my head like a football player and ran back to my cruiser. I grabbed the door handle, opened the door and started to climb into the driver's seat. Right as I put my foot to the floor and was bending down, I looked on top of my cruiser. What did I find? That little spider monkey, holding on to the blue light with every hair on his body blown back and his little forehead full of bugs!

Leo Mudd
1975

ON THE FIRST DAY, THERE WAS LIGHT

The flashlight's a very important piece of equipment to a police officer, especially for officers working the night shift. Let me tell you about the time I first used mine.

It was my first night shift as a rookie cop, and I was determined to ensure that this invaluable tool would be used properly and in accordance with the many hours of training I had received at the academy. I was riding with my training officer, and we were looking for traffic violators.

As I engaged my first violator, I was focused on the proper use of my flashlight. It was all I could think about. I knew it could be used as a "prepared defense weapon." I knew it wasn't just an illumination device. Conscious of this alternate function, I held it firmly in the hand opposite my "gun-hand," standing roadside.

I shined the light on the offender's driver's license as I checked for the proper identification numbers. (After several stops, this would become a routine. But, since this was my first citation, I had to carefully concentrate on every move I slowly made.)

Finally, a long night was ending, and we had made a bunch of stops. After breakfast as we were driving back for shift change, we encountered a speeding motorist. We decided to make one more stop. By then, I was feeling like an experienced professional. I mean, I had **one** complete shift to my new career's credit!

Pulling to proper position behind the motorist, I took the cruiser out of gear. I grabbed my flashlight. I opened the door and dismounted. I walked tall. Reaching "safe position," I handily directed the beam of my flashlight toward the driver's lap and outstretched hand. Then I took the offender's license between the fingers of my "gun-hand." Upon the identification numbers I shined my light.

I noticed a strange look on the driver's face, a curious and dumbfounded sort of expression in his eyes. Then I noticed that bright morning sun in the eastern sky. I was standing there using my flashlight to check those numbers in broad daylight!

"Is this your correct address?" I asked.

"Yes, sir," the man replied, his eyes fixated on my big flashlight.

Shuffling my boots in the roadside gravel, I said, "You never know when there might be an eclipse."

"Yes, sir," he responded. "You're absolutely right."

Looking him square in the face, I said, "Just wait right here, sir. I'll be back in a flash!"

Pretty quick thinking for a cop, I thought, as I strolled on back, with a sense of accomplishment, to the engine's hum and radio noise of my Kentucky State Police cruiser. Mounting my vehicle, I flicked off the light.

Courtesy of Mickey Kipper

BETWEEN A ROCK AND A PRISON

I heard this story recently from a friend out west. One afternoon, a man left work and discovered three men breaking into his pickup truck. The man flagged down my buddy who happened to be patrolling the area, and the officer took off in pursuit. The culprits had fled on foot into an old rock quarry near San Quentin Prison. The officer followed them into the quarry where they tried to hide. Unfortunately, the would-be thieves didn't realize they were inside the prison gates.

Once they figured out where they were, they tried to escape, but bumped into a San Quentin officer who was on his way back to headquarters after practicing at the firing range.

The fools were inside the prison gates and trapped between the police and a San Quentin guard. Needless to say, they were captured.

"Talk about a wrong-way gang!" my buddy said, laughing, as he told me this one.

Courtesy of Cindy Furnare

CUE BALL IN THE POCKET

A good friend told me about a funny thing that happened to him and a partner in Louisville, Ky., some years back. They were working the night shift patrolling the downtown area. It was the smallest beat in the city, and the officers were practically driving in circles looking for some action.

About 10 p.m., they found themselves in a parking lot beside a bar known to be a trouble spot, so they parked and waited for something to happen.

Pretty soon, the bar door flew open and a man ran to a car parked near the officers. He popped the trunk, reached in, took something from the floor and hid it in his pocket. He headed back toward the bar, and my buddy jumped out to question him before any trouble occurred. The man got to the door first, so the officers followed him in. He took one look at the police and headed for the restroom.

When the officers caught up with the man, he had his right hand in his pocket, obviously holding something. My buddy prepared to draw his service revolver as he told the man to bring his hand out very slowly. As the man did, my buddy saw what looked like the ivory handle of a pistol. He readied himself and repeated, "Very slowly now." An ivory cue ball emerged from the pocket. The man was hiding a cue ball! My buddy felt relieved, but a little embarrassed.

The man explained, "The guys at the bar didn't believe me when I told them I had a genuine ivory cue ball."

Courtesy of James H. Simon

THE "COMEBACK" SPEEDER

Here's one I heard from a devoted University of Kentucky Wildcats fan. On his car, he has U.K. bumper stickers, a U.K. license plate, tail lights that read "Wild" on the left and "Cats" on the right, plus brake lights that flash "U.K." when he stops!

He was driving I-75 north out of Knoxville, Tenn., when he took Highway 80 west at London, Ky. Since he had gotten accustomed to the 65 mph speed limit on the interstate, he neglected to slow down when he hit Highway 80. He was going about 70 when the police officer stopped him.

That old boy started writing out a ticket, and my buddy wondered how can he get out of this mess. Then he had a bright idea and said, "Excuse me, officer, are you by chance a Kentucky fan?" The officer just stood there grinning and writing.

"Can I just show you a few things I have on the back of my car?" my buddy asked. The officer still said nothing, just kept writing away. Then my buddy asked, "Do you know Reggie Hansen?"

"The U.K. player? Well, I sure do!" the officer answered.

With that opening, my buddy said, "C'mon, and take a look at this."

The two of them walked to the back of the car, and my friend showed him that whole blue-and-white spectacle of U.K. paraphernalia. Then he said, "How could you possibly write a brother a ticket?"

The officer paused for a moment and said, "Be more careful and slow it down some. Now get out of here!"

Boy, was my friend relieved.

Courtesy of Rev. Vernon W. Harris

A LOT OF BULL

As I travel around the country, I meet a lot of police officers, and we all have one thing in common – at least one embarrassing story. A friend from the Garden State laughed so hard when he told me this one, he choked.

One dark, foggy night, a young state trooper was driving a senior trooper around the rural roads of New Jersey. The old-timer told the recruit, "Listen, kid, I am gonna close my eyes for awhile and catch a few ZZZZZs. Don't stop anyone, just miles and smiles, OK?" "Yes, sir," replied the kid.

After an hour of backroading, the sleeping trooper was abruptly awakened by screeching tires and a tremendous bang. Coming to his senses, the sleepy trooper realized he was covered in what smelled like cow manure. And looking through what used to be his windshield, he saw a large, hairy, brown object three inches from his face. To his astonishment, the "kid" had hit a cow on the foggy roadway. The cow had slid up the hood, smashed the windshield and come to rest three inches from the senior officer's face. Covered in the cow's last bowel movement, the old-timer crawled out through the passenger window to take a gander at the mess. The "deceased," which had only been knocked unconscious, quickly scrambled off the hood and tried to walk away.

Thinking the Sarg would never believe this story, the old-timer decided to put down the "injured" cow. After he discharged a round, the cow charged, and with nowhere to go but up, the officers scrambled onto the damaged cruiser's roof. Just then a motorist came by, only to see the troopers on the roof shooting at a cow which appeared to be holding them at bay. Before they could signal for help, the car suddenly accelerated and disappeared in the fog.

In a few minutes, the cow's owner arrived. To his dismay, he saw his prize-winning cow lying dead beside the troopers' car, one manure-covered trooper and one white-as-a-ghost rookie standing over the carcass, cursing.

Upon their return to the station, the officers were called into the Sarg's office. "What the hell was going on out there?" he demanded. "We had someone stop and complain that two troopers were using the roof of their car for a better vantage point to shoot cows! And what the hell is manure doing all over your uniform?"

A week later, Farmer John stopped by the station with 200 pounds of steak for the pair. He claimed it was the most pitiful sight he had ever seen – one manure-covered trooper and one rookie close to tears. This was the least he could do for them.

Courtesy of J. L. Vincent

SMILE, YOU'RE ON
CANDID (SURVEILLANCE) CAMERA

A few years back, I heard a story about a man who was unknowingly caught by one of those automated speed traps. It measured his speed and photographed his license plate.

Soon he received in the mail a ticket for $40 and a photo of his license plate. Instead of sending the money, he sent a photograph of two $20 bills.

In return, the police department sent him a photograph of a pair of handcuffs!

The man sent the money in pretty quick after that.

Courtesy of Joe Hill

MERRY CHRISTMAS AND SURPRISE!

The other day I heard about a couple of crooks who tried to do a little after-hours Christmas shopping. Here's the way the story goes:

One evening near closing time, the folks working at a Toys R Us store heard voices above their heads. It sounded like two men were hiding up there waiting to rob the store. In fact, the crooks were talking so loudly, the workers could hear them discussing in detail how they were going to do it.

When the police arrived, they found the pair crouched above the ceiling with guns, wire cutters, ski masks, gloves and flashlights.

They were dressed in green and red thinking they would not be noticed.

THE 'TRASHY' LOVE NOTE

A detective buddy of mine in Montgomery, Ala., who works juvenile cases, told me this crazy story:

When he came to work one morning, he was assigned a burglary case. And after gathering what information the dispatcher had, he set out to visit the crime scene.

The homeowners reported their house had been robbed, and then the woman started to giggle. When the detective asked what was funny, she explained that the only things missing were a South Trust Bank watch (worth about $5), two tickets to the Alabama vs. Georgia football game and a bag of candy. She found it strange that the burglars hadn't stolen the television or some of the more expensive items that were readily available.

The detective found it strange too. After asking for permission to search for evidence, he found a sheet of paper wadded into a ball in the kitchen wastebasket. It turned out to be a love letter, and it looked like it had been written by a young girl asking a boy if he liked her.

Now, what makes this crime really stupid is that her name, address and telephone number were written in big bold letters on the top and bottom of the letter!

My buddy found all the missing property at the young girl's home.

BIKE COP

My friend sent in this poem.

I ride my big black bicycle
In traffic every day.
Some think that this is working,
Some think that this is play.

I drive with utmost caution;
At each red light I stop.
For I know that folks are watching
Every move of Bicycle Cop.

I keep my weapon locked in tight
As I ride round and round.
For God forbid I hit a bump,
And it falls on the ground.

We're out in all the weather,
Be it ever hot or cold.
And still I wear my biking shorts,
To show the chicks I'm bold.

I also wear these sexy shades

That folks think are sunglasses.
They're worn not just to fight the sun,
But 'cause it thrills the lasses.

My vest it shall protect me
On my bike or in a mall,
But when I ride, I have it on,
Should a pothole make me fall.

I carry all this shiny gear,
The weight it makes me slow,
But I wouldn't lose a single piece,
'Cause I need them all for show.

When we start our tour of duty,
We shall travel near and far.
I tell everyone I love it,
But I really miss my car.

Courtesy of William A. Connell

REACH OUT AND TOUCH A CAR THIEF

One afternoon, I checked out a stolen car report. The woman owner mentioned that a cellular phone was in the vehicle. When I heard this, I thought, "Well, there's more than one way to catch a thief!"

I dialed the phone's number, and when a man answered, I said I had seen the newspaper advertisement for the car and was interested in buying it. We figured out a place to meet.

When the guy showed up, I arrested him!

Courtesy of Cindy Furnare

ZIP IT UP

This friend of mine was working with a rookie cop the night the trainee earned the nickname "Zipper." Here's how he got it:

My buddy and the trainee made a traffic stop on a suspected drunk driver. The trainee requested the driver's license and registration (which was out-of-state New York), and proceeded to run the license check.

The dispatcher came back asking for a confirmation on the driver's license number, and the trainee repeated it. "Not on file in New York," the dispatcher responded.

My buddy took the license from the trainee. And, trying not to laugh, he informed the rookie that he had just run a check on the suspect's zip code.

Back at the station, the trainee was christened Zipper!

Courtesy of Jim

WHAT KIND OF AN AFFAIR?

I heard a story recently that will make you think before you speak. Seems a young prospective cadet was standing there all nervous being interviewed by a Kentucky State Police officer who asked him, "Have you ever been involved in a community affair?"

The wannabe-cadet dropped his head, gazed up through his eyebrows, paused, then said, "Yes, Ma'am – but only once."

The officer listened attentively as the young man slowly went on to say, "I have been faithful to my wife ever since then."

Remember: Think, then speak.

God bless all police officers, their families and wannabe-cadets too.

Courtesy of Tom Felder

THE BLUE-EYED JACK-O-LANTERN

L et me share a funny story from a friend who had a spooky experience one Halloween night. He was sound asleep after a long night of chasing pranksters and vandals all around town. The ringing phone woke him, and he was dispatched to a traffic accident involving a truck loaded with dog food.

When he arrived at the scene, he found what looked like every dog in town feasting on the spilled food. A large crowd had gathered to watch, so he got out of his cruiser and walked to the mess.

As he moved closer, he noticed people in the crowd laughing and pointing to his vehicle. He turned around to find that someone had placed a jack-o-lantern over the single blue light atop his old cruiser. Everyone was watching that old pumpkin head sequentially flashing blue winks and smiles.

Courtesy of Larry Giles

IT ISN'T NICE TO MOCK OTHERS

S ometimes the craziest things happen. Let me tell you about this one night in particular when I was dispatched to investigate a domestic disturbance. I was accompanied by a sergeant who had a speech impediment. At the scene, the sergeant knocked on the door, and said in a stern voice, "O-o-open the d-d-door!"

There was a long pause. Then a voice from inside replied, "N-n-n-not until y-y-you q-q-quit m-m-making f-fun of m-m-me."

Now, that was an awkward moment, let me tell you! You just can't anticipate such strange encounters. By grace alone, we carry on.

Courtesy of P. J. Lawton

THE MOOSE WHO SNIFFS

A buddy of mine shared this story about working undercover as a military police investigator on a drug-suppression team. His job was to make drug buys. Between assignment, he was living at a military replacement center with hundreds of other soldiers also awaiting their assignments.

He went out for a few beers one night, and began talking to a young soldier who said he enjoyed "partaking of a little herb from time to time." Thinking quickly, my buddy asked the soldier if he might be able to secure some "pieces" of hashish, for which he would be greatly indebted. The soldier left the bar and never returned.

Soon after that, my buddy went on a three-month covert investigation. When it was finished, he was very happy to be out in public again.

Back at the replacement center, he was exercising Moose, a narcotics detector dog. Moose was extremely well-known in the community, since he had been used in literally hundreds of drug searches.

The young soldier from the bar approached my buddy and greeted him: "Hey, long-time-no-see!" Then, whispering he asked, "Are you still looking for those 'pieces'?"

Shocked at how stupid this guy could be, my buddy answered, "Yeah, how much you want for 'em?" It was all he could do not to laugh out loud. A price was agreed upon, and it was only a matter of moments before Moose was sniffing out the drugs in the soldier's possession.

He was arrested and subsequently discharged from the service. In that brief encounter, his rank, position, career and reputation vanished. Just goes to show how dumb it is to mess with drugs.

Courtesy of P. Deming

OIL AND MARIJUANA DON'T MIX

I got a big laugh out of this story a friend from Texas told me the other day. It just goes to show how stupid some criminals really are.

One afternoon, down in San Antonio, my friend was called to a gas station where a woman had taken her car for a routine oil change. What she didn't know was that the mechanic had found a little more than either of them had bargained for. Turns out, when he lifted the hood to check the oil, he found 18 individually wrapped packages of marijuana hidden there.

When the police arrived, the woman admitted she didn't realize the hood would have to be opened for the oil to be changed. Now, if you ask me, that's dumb!

Courtesy of Cindy Furnare

THE TIME WAS NEVER RIGHT

B ack in 1972, when I was working in Clay County, Ky., we used to run road checks in rural areas and would find that many people were driving without operator's licenses.

One afternoon, I was checking cars at a roadblock when a man in his mid-50s pulled to a stop. I asked for his license, and he said he didn't have one. I told him to step back to my cruiser so I could issue him a citation.

As I wrote out the ticket, I asked how long it had been since he had had a driver's license, and he guessed it was since he was 14 or 15 years old. Had he tried to get one since then, I wondered?

"Nope. Guess I never really needed one until right about now."

Courtesy of Carl Elliott

ANYBODY OUT THERE LISTENING?

Iheard this one the other day, and it just goes to show, even undercover, nature calls. A police officer I know and an informant were working to bust a ring of criminals who were getting rid of stolen goods through a local flea market. The two were to purchase some of the goods and then arrest the criminals. The informant was wearing a recording device with a very sensitive microphone because of the noisy flea market.

As the officer and the informant approached the booth, the informant said he had to use the restroom. The officer tried to convince him to wait, but nature was really calling, so the pair headed to the restroom.

Later when the officer was preparing a written report to go along with the tape, he provided some play-by-play action of the bathroom trip: The sound of he and the informant entering the restroom, the informant entering the stall, the squeak of the stall door and then, as the officer described it, "what sounded like Niagra Falls!"

Let me tell you, everyone who read the report while listening to the tape got a kick out of that.

Life as a police officer is humorous, and people can be funny. God, I love this job – even if the pay is terrible sometimes!

Courtesy of Curtis Frame

GOING OUT ON A LIMB

Here's another monkey tale: A dispatcher received an "animal complaint" call from a man who was very upset. His pet spider monkey had climbed a tree and would not come down. He requested the assistance of an officer.

A buddy of mine was dispatched, and when he arrived, he

spotted the little monkey high up in a tree. He tried to call the monkey down. He called and talked and pleaded, but the monkey just sat there staring back at him. So he climbed the tree, crawled out on a limb and attempted to encourage the animal with his nightstick. When he poked, the monkey broke off a twig and poked back. The monkey just kept chattering and poking, but refusing to come out of tree.

Finally, the officer gave a good nudge with his nightstick, and the monkey leaped to the ground with a thud. The little creature walked in circles, dazed and confused, but he was fine.

Needless to say, the officer was suspicious of every animal complaint he received after that. And who wouldn't be?

Courtesy of Elaine Bohne Hornback

TOO MUCH "CENTS"

Here's one I heard from a friend up north the other day. A thief in Providence, R.I., assaulted the driver of an armored vehicle and attempted to escape with four bags of money.

My friend was called to the scene, and, as it turns out, the four bags were filled with $800 – all in pennies! The bags weighed about 40 pounds each.

They were so heavy, my friend was able to run the thief down on foot as he tried to drag the money away.

Courtesy of Cindy Furnare

NOW THAT'S A FLUSHED FACE

Now here's a funny story about a couple of cops working the "dogwatch" for a small department near San Antonio, Texas. One was in desperate need of a "P. R." break when they were dispatched to an alarm sounding at a large, newly constructed home. The front door was open, and as they "cleared" the house, the first officer discovered a bathroom. He decided he could wait no longer. The large, luxurious bathroom was not yet equipped with lights, but he noticed it had two toilets, so he selected the closest one and relieved himself.

After doing his duty, he reached for the handle, but instead, found a strange knob down below the toilet seat. Leaning over, he twisted it with his right hand. Suddenly a stream of liquid gushed up, spraying him in the face – and it wasn't clean water because this was no ordinary toilet.

He yelled for his partner who rushed in, gun drawn. The soggy officer said, "The toilet attacked me!" His partner just stood there laughing. Embarrassed, he swore his partner to secrecy after his first encounter with a "bidet."

Courtesy of Sgt. A. Gonzales

I'LL BELIEVE IT
WHEN PLYWOOD FLIES

Sometimes truth is stranger than fiction! Two young fellows decided to use a pickup truck to haul a number of 4 x 8-foot sheets of plywood. After purchasing the sheets and loading the truck, they discovered the last few sheets were a little above the top of the pickup truck's sides. Unfortunately, they didn't bring any rope to tie down the plywood, and, since it was windy, one of the fellows decided to sit on plywood to prevent it from falling, as they traveled home.

They didn't have far to go, but it was getting late, and the driver wanted to get home as soon as possible so they could put up some of the plywood.

As he was driving down the road, he noticed heavy traffic ahead, and decided he'd better slow down. Suddenly something flew over the top of his truck. He realized it was one of the sheets of plywood with his friend hanging on for dear life.

A motorist traveling the opposite direction noticed something coming toward his vehicle, so he swerved, but the UFO bounced off the roof of his car, and onto the roadway behind him.

A second motorist saw the object bounce off the car ahead of him, and fall onto the road in front of his car. He couldn't stop in time, and ran over the plywood and its rider. The second motorist told me, "I couldn't do anything to avoid him. He was flying through the air, like on a flying carpet, bouncing off car roofs, and it was just like he aimed right at my car." And I *believe* him!

Courtesy of Jim Mentzer

GOOD MANNERS ARE FINE, BUT . . .

I had a big laugh when a buddy of mine from Philadelphia told me about a near-blunder he made.

The city was plagued with bank robberies. One district, in particular, was being hit three and four times a week. To remedy the situation, officers in the district were assigned to visit locations and sign bank logs several times each day.

My buddy, an experienced officer, was making his assigned rounds and parked near a bank which had already been robbed several times during the previous year. He left his cruiser out of sight, dismounted and walked toward the front entrance.

When he arrived at the swinging glass doors, he pushed just as a man exiting also pushed. Now, my friend is a big man, so the door stopped flat against him. Being considerate, my buddy pulled the door open, held it for the man and wished him a pleasant day. He told me the guy looked nervous, but thought it was just because he had collided with a cop.

My buddy entered the bank, and walked to the desk where he was supposed to sign the log. He couldn't understand why everyone was staring at him as he cheerfully greeted the guard. Then the guard informed my friend that he had just held the door for a man who had robbed the tellers at gunpoint and made off with a large sum of cash!

Well, the officer immediately radioed dispatchers and, fortunately, the man was apprehended just a few blocks away. Needless to say, he was embarrassed when he had to explain the order of events to the F.B.I.

Courtesy of Bob Ralston

CRUISER ON THE LOOSE

I know a cop out in California who had one wild experience as a rookie. His story goes like this:

My friend, a California Highway Patrol officer, stopped a motorist on one the Hollywood Freeway's steep grades, approached the driver's side, and requested her vehicle registration and license.

He noticed the woman was looking in astonishment back to where his cruiser was parked. Following her eyes, he turned to see his black-and-white rolling backwards down the shoulder and into traffic. He chased after it as it crossed all four lanes, and he reached it just before it crashed into the center divider. Needless to say, traffic on the congested freeway had come to a stop as surprised motorists watched the officer running after his car.

He drove back to the shoulder, but this time set the brake. Trying not to look too embarrassed as he returned the woman's license, he said, "I need a donut."

Courtesy of John Yeaw

TRY OUR KANGAROO BUFFET

I heard a funny story about a cop up in New York City. I guess you never know what you'll find up there.

The officer was working the midnight to 8 a.m. shift in a fashionable business district. Making his rounds on foot, he had checked all the businesses for open doors and was relaxing when he heard a noise coming from the rear of the stores. It was the sound of garbage cans being clanged together, a loud banging series of crashes.

The officer thought the noise might be coming from behind a Chinese restaurant, and, suspecting a break-in, he proceeded to the rear of the restaurant with his flashlight blazing and gun drawn. When he got there, you won't believe what he found. A kangaroo foraging through the trash! He radioed this information to his dispatcher.

Later on, he learned the desk officer on duty thought he was drunk when he made the call. And everybody back at the station thought he had gone crazy.

But, actually, the man was correct. A kangaroo had been lost during a movie shoot just a few days earlier and must have gotten hungry. The next day the animal was captured by a motorcycle cop who lassoed him on a golf course like a New York cowboy. It just goes to show, you never know what to expect.

Courtesy of M. E. Riederer

WET AND WILD PATROL

I had a rather embarrassing experience when I was a young officer.

Out on patrol with my training officer, I spotted a man crouched in the rear corner of a shopping mall. It was after midnight, and he looked suspicious to me. I thought I'd better check this out. We parked our cruiser and observed him for some time before deciding to see what he was up to.

Being the rookie, I approached him and shouted, "Police officer! Don't move!"

Startled, he jumped back and turned to see who had scared him. Before I knew what was going on, that ol' boy was tinkling all over my leg. Man, did I feel silly. My training officer just laughed and laughed. We arrested the man for being intoxicated and urinating in public.

Back at the station, the man said, "I've been arrested for pissing off the police, but never for pissing ON the police!"

I didn't think it was funny when the cops nicknamed me "Drippy." And it took a while to lose that name, let me tell you.

Courtesy of Jim Gillman

WHEN HONESTY DOESN'T PAY

Here's one I heard recently from a cop across the ocean: A friend of mine in Belgium was questioning a man suspected of robbing a jewelry store in the city of Liege. When the officer asked him where he was at the time of the crime, the suspect said there was no way he could have done it.

"Why?" the officer asked, and the guy said because he was busy breaking into a school at the same time!

My friend laughed, and then gladly arrested the crook for the school break-in.

Courtesy of Cindy Furnare

LOOK BEFORE YOU LEAP

I know a police officer who got himself into a slippery situation one rainy night. My friend and his partner responded to a "violent domestic" call.

After parking the cruiser, they started toward the house, which was surrounded by a split rail fence. My buddy got the bright idea to leap the fence while his partner provided cover. He readied himself, drew a deep breath and got off to a running start. He planted his hand atop the fence, vaulted into the air – and the fence came crashing down.

Lying on the wet ground in the pouring rain and dark of night, he looked around and realized he was only a few feet from the end of the fence. He could have easily gone around it. His partner stood there laughing out loud. It just goes to show, always look before you leap!

Courtesy of Don Siddall

SNOWING THE POLICE DOESN'T PAY

One snowy night, I was dispatched to a burglary scene at a convenience store. When I arrived, witnesses told me the thieves had loaded their vehicle with stolen goods and sped off just minutes before. In their rush to leave, the suspects had backed into a snowbank at the edge of the parking lot.

Believe it or not, I found a perfect imprint of their license plate in the snow, and soon made a successful arrest, you might say, with a little help from nature!

Courtesy of Mike Pittman

SAY IT AGAIN, SAM

Here's one I heard that could have ended badly if not for my buddy's Spanish-speaking partner.

The officer was patrolling with a new trainee. The trainee spoke some Spanish, but my friend spoke none. As they were checking out a reported disturbance, they ran into a man with a gun.

After taking cover on opposite sides of their cruiser, my buddy yelled out, "Drop the gun!" The man didn't respond, so he tried again, yelling louder, "Drop the gun!" The man, who seemed to be of Spanish descent still didn't respond.

So the officer called to the trainee, "Tell him to drop the gun."

The trainee shouted, "Drop the gun!"

"No. Tell him in Spanish!" The suspect responded immediately, and he was arrested, but it was a close call!

Courtesy of Mike Alexander

WHAT A GUILTY CONSCIENCE!

When I was a younger and electronic ignitions had just been added to cars, my department had a cruiser that would quit for no reason. Just die right there on the spot. One night the darn thing quit on me, so I called for a tow, and another officer was sent to pick me up.

I radioed the officer to let him know that I was under the brow of a hill and off the road. I said as soon as I saw him at the top of the hill, I would switch on my overheads to let him know where I was.

Well, pretty soon I saw what I thought was the officer coming, so I switched on my lights. As soon as I did, the car braked sharply and wound up halfway in a nearby ditch.

As I started to the car, a man crawled out, and began walking toward me, yelling, "You got me! I was speeding! I guess I deserve it! I shouldn't have been flying like that !"

Pretty funny, I thought.

Courtesy of Rocky Clayton

VISIT THE CROSSBAR MOTEL

My buddy tells this funny story about two drunks outside a Texas bar. He was passing a West Texas bar when a couple of drunks staggered out and stumbled over to the edge of the road. They waved their hands and started whistling and shouting, "Taxi!" He stopped up his cruiser. The fools jumped into the back seat and asked to be taken to a motel.

Well, he delivered them to jail instead, and it wasn't until they were standing in the booking room that they noticed they were in the wrong "motel."

Courtesy of Dave Spilman

SOMETIMES YOU SHOULDN'T HELP A MOTORIST

An officer I know had an embarrassing thing happen to him back in the early 1960s.

He was pulling the "graveyard" shift in Lake City, Mich., when he came across a stalled car with three young men in it. He got their I.D.'s and ran a license check, but in those days, it took six or seven hours to get registration information back.

The boys seemed okay, so my buddy helped them push the car over to a nearby downgrade, and it started. They drove back up the hill to thank the officer for his help. "Very polite boys," my friend recalled.

The next morning his home phone rang, and it was his superior wondering which way the boys had traveled. Turns out the car was stolen. Needless to say, my buddy heard about that one for a long time.

Courtesy of Dave Bremer

OOPS! WRONG I.D.

One night, I was dispatched to investigate a suspicious vehicle parked in a woman's driveway. When I arrived, the truck was still in gear and running, and driver was sound asleep with his head on the wheel and his foot still on the brake pedal. I reached in, turned the ignition off, and then tried to roust the man. He was out cold, and snoring loud enough to wake the neighborhood. I guessed he was drunk.

It took 20 minutes of shaking the guy and using my loud speaker to wake him. As he stumbled out, he said, "Is there a problem, officer?"

I asked if he knew where he was, and he replied, "I'm home."

When I asked for his driver's license, he dug way down deep into his pocket, pulled out a sandwich bag, handed it to me, and said, "Here you go!" The bag was filled with marijuana.

So after laughing a bit, I arrested him for DUI and possession of marijuana, and hauled him down to the county jail.

Courtesy of William Niemi

SURPRISE, SURPRISE, SURPRISE

N ow, crazy things happen in court all the time, but I saw something one time that you will not believe. A drug possession defendant on trial claimed his rights had been violated, since he had been searched without a warrant.

The prosecutor claimed the officer did not need a warrant since a "bulge," which could have been a gun, had been spotted in the defendant's pocket. Now, this made sense to me, but what happened next was just crazy!

The defendant, who was wearing the very same jacket in court that day, claimed this argument was nonsense. He then handed his jacket over to the judge for examination. The judge checked the jacket and discovered a package of cocaine in the pocket. His Honor was laughing so hard he needed a five-minute recess to compose himself.

Courtesy of Cindy Furnare

YOU WANT THE HOURLY OR NIGHTLY RATE?

L ate one night, I was flagged down by a group of motorists who needed help with an inebriated woman. She was so drunk and insistent upon driving that her friends had taken away her car keys and thrown them into a roadside ditch. She was crawling around on the newly tarred road, sweeping her hands across the pavement, hoping to find her keys. The pretty white pant suit she was wearing was all but ruined at the knees.

When she figured out that I planned to arrest her, she begged me to go with her to a motel. When I said I couldn't do that, she started yelling and screaming, slobbering and crying. She became so loud and angry that I nearly had to restrain her.

Finally, I told her that if she would quiet down, I'd take her to a nice motel. She calmed down, smiled and settled nicely into the back seat of my cruiser.

When we arrived at the jail, I escorted her inside. She sauntered right up to the duty officer and said in a drunken voice, "We'd like a room, please."

DEER "HANG OUT"

S ome fellow officers pulled a pretty funny prank on a cop I know in Atlanta. Here's how it happened:

My friend works the day shift in rural Fulton County where it's mostly farmland and woods. There are deer in the area., but fortunately in Georgia, the deer are pretty small. Every now and then, though, officer get called about an accident involving one.

One day, there was an accident, and a fireman took the dead animal with him for the meat. At the fire station, which is a favorite police hang-out, one of the deer's legs was laying around and fell into the hands of a prankster. He placed the leg in the trunk of my buddy's cruiser, making it look like a deer was in the trunk.

Well, some citizens were offended, and the complaints came rolling in. The local people were appalled that one of "Fulton County's Finest" was driving around with a dead deer in his trunk.

Not knowing what he was carrying around, my buddy couldn't understand why his lieutenant gave him a severe tongue-lashing.

Courtesy of Dan Nable

NO SIR, THAT'S NOT MINE!

I was on patrol one night when I was called to investigate a burglary. I drove to the location and when I got there, I found the screens had been cut, the glass in a back door was shattered, and there was blood on the glass.

As I searched the area, I saw a drainage ditch that went under the road. It looked like a good hiding place, so I walked over to have a look. Sure enough, there were two teenage boys hiding there.

I brought them to my cruiser, handcuffed and patted them down. I found burglary tools, and one of the boys had a fresh cut on his hand.

I asked him, "How did you get that blood on your hand?"

He looked me square in the eye and said, "Oh, that's not mine!"

I took them to the station, and everybody busted out laughing when he told the same story. We all cracked up because he just stood there like a "deer caught in headlights!"

Courtesy of Margie Campbell

THE INVISIBLE SISTER

L et me tell you about a wild one that occurred a while back. I was on patrol when I received a call to report to a house where an elderly woman had been assaulted. I raced to the scene at breakneck speed using lights and sirens

Arriving within minutes of her 911 call, I found the woman in her nightgown, and it was obvious she had been assaulted. Her nose was bleeding, and her face was swollen and cut. When I asked what happened, she said her sister had beaten her up.

"Where is your sister now?" I asked.

"She's in my garage. "

I rushed to the garage, looked around, but nobody was there. It was completely empty. So I went back into the house and told the woman her sister was gone.

She said, "No, she's still in the garage."

"Ma'am, there is nobody out ...."

She interrupted, "C'mon, I'll show you!" We walked to the garage and she pointed to a corner. "There!"

"Ma'am, there's nobody there. It's empty."

Growing irritated, she said, "Are you blind, officer? She is standing right in front of you!"

At this point a little light went on in my head, and I said, "Tell me about your sister, Ma'am."

"She always used to beat me! Even before she died."

"When did she die, Ma'am?"

"Seven years ago."

To this day I wonder how that woman received her injuries. Guess I'll never know.

Courtesy of Chris Beaty

IS IT "I BEFORE E, EXCEPT AFTER C?"

I got a kick out of this story I heard from a friend down in Texas about a bunch of dumb drug smugglers. The smugglers in El Paso had attempted to use a propane tanker truck to bring marijuana into the United States from Mexico. The truck was rigged so that, if inspected, propane gas would be released from all of the external valves. The tank contained 6,240 pounds of marijuana.

Now that's pretty clever, but not clever enough. The criminals had misspelled the name of the gas company on the side of the vehicle. My friend checked out the company and made an easy arrest. Some people just have no sense!

Courtesy of Cindy Furnare

GIVING THE SHIRT OFF YOUR BACK FOR A CIGARETTE

I remember a case when a guy decided to break into a gas station through a window and steal all the cigarettes. He took off his shirt and wrapped it around a boulder to muffle the noise of breaking glass. Sure enough, the glass broke and he got away with all the cigarettes.

When I arrived at the scene, I found the shirt still wrapped around that old rock, and in the pocket was the man's wallet with his driver's license and Social Security card. It was just a matter of arresting him.

Courtesy of Nicholas Glaser

THREE IS ENOUGH, THANKS

I heard a funny story the other day from a police officer in New York state. If you think police work is tough, try being mom to three young children.

My friend was working as a dispatcher one night when he got a wild call. A woman shouted, "I can't take these kids anymore! I could just smash 'em!"

In his best police manner, the officer said, "Calm down, Ma'am. I don't think you really want to hurt your children."

"They're driving me crazy! " she yelled. I'm gonna kill 'em!"

"Ma'am, please tell me where you're calling from."

She answered, "You don't understand! Three kids are enough to drive you crazy!"

"Now, get hold of yourself. Is there someone who can come over and help you with them? You know, my wife and I have three kids, and they can be difficult at times, but she always finds a way to handle it. Where are you calling from?"

Then the woman said, "Don't you know who this is?"

"Huh?"

"This is your wife!"

Boy, did he feel foolish. His wife knew he hadn't recognized her voice, so she decided to let him have it.

Courtesy of Ken Bergmann

PERSONAL CONTACT

I t was my first day as a Kentucky State Trooper, and I was writing my first speeding ticket. I was a bundle of nerves. I sat on the passenger side of the cruiser writing the ticket as my training officer watched.

When I finished, he asked to see the ticket to make sure

everything was properly filled out. After examining my work, there was a long silence. Then he got very excited, and said, "What an amazing coincidence! This guy has the same name and address as you."

Boy, did I feel stupid! I had written that first ticket to myself.

Courtesy of Mickey Kipper

UNWANTED GHOSTLY GUESTS

I heard this good one from a friend out west. He and his partner were working the night shift, and things were quiet until they got dispatched to a "burglary in progress." The caller said there were people in her house.

The officers drove to the mobile home park and found her lot. Since it had been snowing, they looked around for footprints but couldn't find any. They knocked on the door and an elderly lady answered. My buddy asked, "What's the problem?"

She turned and pointed to an empty couch, and said, "The two sitting there!"

"Where, Ma'am?" his partner asked.

"Right there! Arrest them!" she demanded.

My buddy walked over to the couch and said firmly, "All right, come with me. You're under arrest. Let's go!" Then he led the imaginary pair out to the cruiser and pretended to place them in the back, all the time hoping she didn't still see them sitting on the couch.

His partner said, "Ma'am, we'll take them to jail now." They never heard from her again.

DEPOSIT CHECK—NOT STUB

Several years back, I responded to a "bank holdup in progress" call. But by the time I arrived, the robbers had already fled.

I started interviewing witnesses and gathering evidence. As I was putting the holdup note in an evidence bag, I noticed it was a pay stub with a name, address and Social Security number right there on the back. I thought to myself, "Is this too good to be true?"

It wasn't. When an armed robbery unit and I went to the address, sure enough, we had our man.

Courtesy of Darrell Osborne

SO CLOSE AND YET SO FAR

A buddy of mine who works out in Texas told me about a funny chase he went on one night.

He was patrolling a desolate area of west Texas when he noticed a spotlight down by the Rio Grande River. From his vantage point, he could see the light clearly, but out there it takes a long time to get from Point A to Point B by car. Since there had been a lot of poaching complaints, he decided to investigate.

As he got closer, he could make out a truck and three men. He drove toward them with his lights off until he was very close and then switched on his headlights and overhead flashers. He said the men got the surprise of their lives when his lights flashed on. Unfortunately, even though they were within shouting distance, they were on Mexico's side of the Rio Grande.

He figured they must have had a real good laugh, too.

Courtesy of Fernando Cervantes

POLICE PREVENTS PRAYERFUL PAUSE

Often times as police officers, we must deal with death. I remember a time I responded to a call and found a man had died accidentally near his home. His widow was there and she insisted on staying.

Experience had taught me that it was not uncommon for family members to faint in such stressful circumstances, so I put my arm around her shoulder in a fatherly fashion to provide support and comfort.

When her knees buckled twice, I tightened my grasp. Finally, the third time her knees began to bend, she looked me straight in the eye and said, "For God's sake, will you let me kneel down and pray over him?"

TALKING OUT OF TURN

Here's a crazy scene I saw in court one day. A man was on trial for the robbery of a convenience store. He had fired his attorney and chosen to defend himself. And he was doing a pretty fair job until the store manager, who he had robbed, took the stand. The manager testified that the defendant was, in fact, the robber.

When the defendant heard this, he leaped from his seat and accused the store manager of lying. He shouted, "I should have blown your (expletive) head off!" The defendant paused, then continued, "I mean, if I'd been the one who was there."

The jury required 20 minutes to convict the defendant and suggested a 30-year sentence.

If you ask me, that's pretty funny.

Courtesy of Cindy Furnare

A HOLE IN ONE "BAG"

O ne of the craziest calls I ever had was to investigate a snake in a woman's garden. When I got there, sure enough, a snake about 18 inches long was sunning itself.

There was all kinds of talk back and forth between the dispatcher and me. A snake expert was consulted to determine just what kind of snake it was and how it should be handled. When the snake was judged harmless, I caught it with my bare hands and placed it in a bag.

I decided to take it to a snake handler who lived nearby. To make the reptile comfortable, I poked a hole in the bag, hoping it would help the snake breathe more easily. Well, about halfway to the snake handler's, I looked down and saw that big old snake slithering right into the ventilation system of my cruiser.

Needless to say, it took a brave mechanic to go in later and find it.

Courtesy of Richard Wall

RUNAWAY VEHICLE

A while back, I was dispatched to an accident at a circular interchange – a big 10-lane nightmare governed by stop signs. It was rush hour and traffic was bumper-to-bumper.

When I got there, two cars were in the center of the circle, and they were hooked together at the bumpers because one had rear-ended the other. A man was jumping on the bumpers trying to unhook the cars.

I asked him to please stop jumping on the cars, and he replied, "I got locked out of my car when I got out." I told him to relax and I would take care of the problem, but he just kept jumping on the cars. I walked over, took his arm and led him to the side of the road where I told him to sit down and wait because the wrecker was on its way.

As I was interviewing the other driver, I looked back and, sure enough, the man was jumping on the bumpers again. I called to another officer to get him back to the side of the road. Right about then, the cars separated, and he screamed, "I did it!"

He really did have it. His car started moving in reverse at a very fast speed because the fool had left it running and in gear! And it was heading straight for the other officer. He jumped out of the way, but his cruiser wasn't so lucky. It was nailed broadside. Actually, this wasn't altogether bad, since if the patrol car hadn't been there, the runaway car would have sped into traffic.

I wasn't sure what to do with the owner of the car, and then he said, "I just remembered, I have a spare key in my wallet." I wrote him a ticket. What else could I do!

Courtesy of William A. Connell

BYRD WATCHING

A friend of mine had a scary experience one night on patrol. He was working the "graveyard" shift when he happened across a car parked near what was supposed to be an abandoned house in a secluded part of town. He radioed the dispatcher that he would be checking the house, all the while he was remembering his nearest backup was 15 minutes away.

Slowly, he approached the car. It was empty, but the hood was still warm, so he knew someone was close. He went back to his car and radioed in the plate number, but it was clean. He decided to check the house.

He carefully walked around, checking all the doors and

windows. Everything was locked until he came to a door in the rear. He twisted the handle, keeping his flashlight fixed on the doorway. Suddenly, there was the sound of shuffling and the door popped wide open!

A man was staring him right in the face. He went for his gun, knowing it was too late. "Put your hands where I can see them!" he screamed. The man didn't move. He just stood there with a smile on his face.

Falling backwards, the officer pulled up his gun, ready to squeeze the trigger if need be. Seconds seemed like hours. Gathering his wits, he realized it wasn't a man at all, but a life-size cardboard cutout of basketball player Larry Byrd! He looked to see what the movement had been, and found a friendly dog sitting just behind the figure.

Turns out some college kids were moving into the place and had already brought their dog and some of their belongings.

My buddy said, "Thank God, they weren't there to see me nearly blow away Larry Byrd!"

Courtesy of Mike Gerr

A UNIQUE ROADSIDE ADOPTION

One day driving down the highway, I noticed a tractor trailer stopped on the roadside and a car parked on an exit ramp with a woman standing beside it. Assuming there had been an accident, I stopped to help.

Well, it turned out the truck had simply broken down near the exit. So, I wondered what in the world this woman was doing. When I approached, she said, "Officer, there's an iguana under my car."

"Pardon me, Ma'am?"

"There's an iguana under my car." I looked and sure enough there was an iguana – big and green and ugly!

"I want to take it home," she explained. "Don't worry, I

love them and I will care for it."

Being a dutiful servant, I crawled around and caught the creature for her. Just another day on the job.

Courtesy of P. Starr

BETTER LATE THAN NEVER

My buddy, a cop in California, told me this story which I thought was pretty funny.

He was working in Burbank at the communications desk one night when a "break-in" alarm call came in from a local stereo store. It was late, and the shift was under-manned, so there was nobody to send to the scene right away. He laid the report aside until a unit was available.

Suddenly he realized 15 minutes had passed and he'd better find someone to check out the alarm. He dispatched a unit, advising them of the delay so they could watch for suspects on the way.

When the officers got there, a window had been broken with a cement block, so they entered the building to search for the burglars. They moved in slowly, guns drawn. Nobody seemed to be there, so they started to fill out the burglary report, figuring the crooks were long gone.

One of the officers then noticed a storage room he hadn't checked. He walked over, opened the door and pointed his weapon, saying jokingly, "I see you there. Come out with your hands up!" To his surprise, a man walked out and surrendered. A second man was captured on the roof.

Turns out the burglars had fled the scene after breaking the window, but when no police arrived, they figured the security stickers were for show, so they returned to clean out the loot.

My buddy felt better when he heard the news. I guess it's better late than never.

THE LONG ARM OF THE LAW

An old boy who worked in rural Kentucky back in the 1940s told me a good one the other day. When he was sheriff of Breckinridge County, he was awakened by a phone call in the middle of the night. The caller was a prominent member of the community, and she was very upset. Seems a drunk had stumbled into her home and made his bed on her couch.

When my friend arrived, sure enough, the man was resting peacefully. Since the sheriff didn't recognize the man, he decided to take him to jail. He reached down, pulled on the man's arm to wake him up, and the arm came right off!

The man finally woke up, replaced his arm and got a trip to jail.

Courtesy of Nell (Bennett) Smith

ANYONE ORDER WINE?

A friend of mine who taught at Morehead State University in eastern Kentucky back in the 1970s told me this crazy story.

He had eaten dinner at a popular winery and enjoyed the wine so much, he decided to buy a case. He was driving home to Morehead in his pickup when a Kentucky State Police officer stopped him for speeding.

Now, my buddy had just heard about a cop who had been transferred to the western part of the state after harassing the president of Morehead. So when the officer walked up to his truck to write the speeding ticket and asked about the case of wine, my quick-thinking buddy said, "I'm taking it to the president of Morehead State who's having a party tonight." As the officer listened, my friend continued, "I'm sorry I was speeding, but I'm late and I'm sure he's pretty mad by now. I really don't want him to be mad at me, you know?"

The officer looked at him for a minute, then went to his car and talked to the dispatcher as my buddy watched, thinking he was in big trouble now for lying.

The officer returned to the truck and said, "Follow me." Before he knew what was going on, my friend found himself being escorted at high speed right to the university president's house – flashing lights and all.

Now my buddy was terrified, wondering how much trouble he would be in when the cop sat there and watched him trying to take the wine into the president's house. But, luckily, the officer waved and sped off. My friend waited a few minutes, and headed for home thinking that was a close one!

Courtesy of George Harper

WHEN A HELPING HAND ISN'T

Now, here's an embarrassing moment that happened to a buddy of mine just a while back. He received his "bolo" sheet at the start of his shift one night, glanced over it quickly and went to work

Out on patrol, he spotted a small station wagon with the hood up, and pulled over to offer help to the man and woman standing beside it. He quickly figured out they needed a jump, so he pulled the cables out of his trunk and got them going. Then he remembered seeing something about a station wagon on the "bolo" sheet. As the couple drove away, he checked it out, and, sure enough, they were driving a stolen car.

He called for backup, and luckily was able to chase them down. Boy, did he feel dumb. The other officers kidded him, but agreed not to mention his assistance to the pair in their report.

ROUND-UP TIME!

During my first year with the Kentucky State Police, while assigned to the Mayfield post, I was called to investigate an animal complaint one evening. Livestock had escaped from a field, and the person who called thought they might cause an accident. This was a routine call in the western part of the state. It usually turned out to be a wandering horse or cow, and it was just a matter of rounding the critter up and getting it back to where it belonged.

I arrived at the scene to find a neighbor guarding a bunch of pigs in his front yard. His house sat right on a dangerous curve on a dark stretch of highway, so it was important to keep the animals off the road both for their sake and the sake of oncoming cars. These pigs were huge and would have totaled a car if struck at high speed. It was a wild and potentially dangerous situation.

Now I didn't know much about pig-herding back then – and still don't – but I was pretty sure these animals could be hazardous to my health if enraged. I wasn't sure how to get them back into their pen without getting attacked or causing them to run out on the road. And I sure didn't want to deal with an accident. Then, an idea hit me. I grabbed my riot baton. I figured I could ward off any attacking pigs before they got too close.

So, there I was in riot gear on the side of the highway in the middle of a bunch of fat old pigs. I felt pretty silly standing there in full polished brass uniform – complete with bulletproof vest – on a hot night chasing down pigs.

I set out flares to warn approaching cars, and gave the neighbor's wife my flashlight to help slow down traffic. I set my blue lights flashing atop my cruiser. Then, I opened the gate to the nearby pen and went to work corralling pigs.

Cars were slowly passing by, maneuvering through the pigs. People were laughing at me chasing those critters around with my riot stick, and doing my best to guide them into their pen. Let me tell you, I must have looked like a real fool. I sure felt like one, but I kept on pushing to get the job done.

Finally, there was one pig left. I had him cornered, nearly into the pen, when he squared off and charged right at me! I jumped to the side and that old pig turned. I think he must have felt sorry for me. He snorted, paused, then ran right into the pen. I shut the gate, packed up my equipment, got in my cruiser and drove off.

Back at the post, the other officers had business cards made up for me that read:

Pork Retention Officer
Office of Livestock Affairs
(Member Ketchum & Fetchum
Livestock Welfare League)
1-800-EAT-PORK

I suppose I'll never live that one down. The funny thing is that's the only time I ever had occasion to use my riot gear. Well, at least the training paid off in the end.

Courtesy of Tom Atkin

AN ASPIRIN A DAY
KEEPS THE ALIASES AWAY

I know a guy who works as a probation officer, so he deals with some rough characters. Some dumb ones too.

One day, he was interviewing a criminal, and he asked, "Do you have any nicknames or aliases?"

The man slowly dropped his head, and thought real hard for a moment to make sure he gave the correct answer. "Well, I've got a lot of stomach problems."

Courtesy of Mikki M. Flowers

10-8

A man broke into a bank's basement through a street-level window, and cut himself in the process. He soon realized that, one, he couldn't get to the money from where he was, two, he couldn't climb back out the window through which he had entered, and, three, he was bleeding pretty badly. So he found a phone and dialed 911 for help.

A young woman was arrested in Lake City, Fla., for the robbery of a Howard Johnson Motel. She was armed with only an electric chain saw, which was not plugged in.

In Virginia, two men went to a new home site to steal a refrigerator. After struggling to remove the appliance, they loaded it into their pickup and promptly got the truck stuck in the mud.

So these "brain surgeons" decided to return the refrigerator. They hauled it back into the house and then realized they had locked the keys in the truck. So they left on foot.

The Ann Arbor (Mich.) News' crime column reported that a man walked into a Ypsilanti Burger King at 7:50 a.m., flashed a gun and demanded cash.

The clerk turned him down, explaining he couldn't open the cash register without a food order. Then when the man ordered onion rings, the clerk said they were only serving breakfast. The frustrated man walked out.

According to New York City police, a man was charged with assault for fondling the wrong woman. Seems he had arranged a visit from a callgirl, and then his live-in girlfriend arrived home early.

He decided to intercept Brandy, the callgirl, in the building's lobby, have sex with her and then return to the apartment before his girlfriend suspected anything.

When he saw a good-looking woman in the lobby, he nudged her into a side hallway, fondled her while displaying a $50 bill and saying, "You know you want it. You know you'll do anything for it."

The woman turned out to be an assistant district attorney from Brooklyn.

A Texas man convicted of robbery worked out a deal to pay $9,600 in damages rather than serve a prison sentence. For the payment, he gave the court a forged check. He got 10 years.

A South Carolina man walked into a police station, dropped a bag of cocaine on the counter, informed the desk sergeant that it was a substandard cut and asked that the person who sold it to him be arrested immediately.

A nervous thief walked into a convenience store, placed a $20 bill on the counter and asked for change. When the clerk opened the cash drawer, the man pulled a gun and demanded all the cash in the register, which the clerk promptly provided. The man then fled, leaving his $20 bill on the counter.

The total amount of cash he got from the store? Fifteen dollars.

In Indiana, a man demanded the grocery store clerk give him all the store's cash. The cashier did as he was told, and the man fled—leaving his wallet on the counter.

An escapee from the Washington, D.C., jail accompanied his girlfriend to her robbery trial. After he left for lunch, the woman decided she needed him, so she had him paged throughout the courthouse
Police officers in the building recognized the name and arrested him when he returned—in a stolen car.

A man successfully broke into a bank, and stole—are you ready for this?—its video camera as it was recording him. Since the videotape recorder was located elsewhere in the bank, officials had a tape of the thief who took their camera.

A hapless thief entered a drugstore, pulled a gun, announced he was robbing the place and promptly pulled a plastic bag over his head. Then he realized he had forgotten to cut eyeholes in it.

A party guest had too much to drink, and his friends pleaded with him to let them take him home. But he refused, saying he only lived a mile away.
About five blocks from the party, police stopped him for weaving and asked him to walk the line. Just then, their radio reported a robbery in progress at a home nearby, so they ordered the party animal to wait until they returned. He did briefly, then decided to go home.
Once there, he told his wife he was going to sleep and to tell anyone looking for him that he was in bed all day with the flu.

Several hours later when police arrived, the woman repeated what her husband had said. But they had his driver's license, so they asked to see his car. When she opened the garage door, there sat a police car—with the lights still flashing.

This true story was told by the driver at his first AA meeting, according to a newspaper report.

Following an armored truck accident, which had dumped money on the street, investigating police learned that some of the cash was already being redistributed. An officer at the scene reported that "one man had grabbed a considerable amount of cash in a bag, took it to his house, threw it in the living room and then ran back to the scene to scoop up more. When he returned home, his house had been burglarized."

While on patrol in Bowling Green, Ky., in the early 1960s, I was sent to assist a woman motorist. Arriving at the intersection, I found a car with its hood open and what I thought was the maddest woman in the world standing beside it.

It seems she had been sitting at a red light and when the light changed the car in front of her didn't move, so she blew her horn. The man driving that car got out, walked back to her car, open its hood (since in those days hoods didn't latch) and used his pocket knife to cut her horn wires.

I wanted to laugh, but looking at the-maddest-woman-in-the-world's face suggested that wouldn't be a good idea. And my explanation that I couldn't do anything without a plate number or a description of the car caused her to totally flip out. I was lucky she didn't attack me then and there.

One night a police officer was staking out a particularly rowdy bar for possible DUI violations. At closing time, he watched a fellow stumble out of the bar, trip over the curb, and try his keys in five different cars before finding his. Then he sat in the front seat fumbling around for several minutes. In the meantime, the other customers left the bar and drove off.

Finally the "drunk" started his engine and began to pull away.

The police officer stopped him, read him his rights and administered a breathalyzer test. The results showed the man hadn't been drinking.

The puzzled officer demanded to know how that could be.

The driver replied, "Tonight, I'm the designated decoy!"

Two Kentucky men tried to pull the front off a cash machine by running a chain from the machine to the bumper of their pickup. Instead of pulling the front panel off, they pulled the bumper off the truck. Scared, they left the scene and drove home, leaving the chain still attached to the cash machine, their bumper still attached to chain and the truck's license plate attached to the bumper.

An Arizona company called Guns for Hire stages gunfights for western movies. One day they received a call from a woman who wanted to have her husband killed. Instead, she received four and one-half years in jail.

A German tourist, supposedly on a golf holiday in England, arrived at customs with his golf bag. As he made idle chatter about golf, customs officials realized he didn't know what a "handicap" was. So they asked him to demonstrate his swing, which he did—backwards. A substantial amount of narcotics was found in the bag.

One night while working the midnight shift in Bristol Township, Pa., I was asked to sit at an intersection while the electric company shut down all power to the area to upgrade the lines. I was told it wouldn't take more than an hour. Three hours later the crew wasn't even halfway done, and I could hear Mother Nature calling with a roar. I explained my dilemma to the foreman, and he assured me it wouldn't take much longer.

My shift was coming to an end, traffic was beginning to pick up and my replacement was nowhere to be seen. I had to do something FAST, so I drove to a nearby store only to find it closed. Then I remembered the rescue squad nearby, so I headed for it.

I could only wonder what drivers were thinking as they pulled off the road as I passed them with full lights and siren. I still laugh when I remember the "accident" I almost had.

A police officer had a perfect hiding place to watch for speeders. One day, however, he discovered a problem. Standing near the road well ahead of his perfect hiding spot was a 10-year-old boy with a huge handpainted sign that read: "RADAR TRAP AHEAD."

A little more investigative work led the officer to the boy's accomplice—another boy positioned about 100 yards beyond the radar trap with a sign reading "TIPS," and a bucketfull of change at his feet.

CHECK-IT-OUT

Here's a funny thing that happened to a cop I know in Detroit:

My buddy was demonstrating his squad car computer equipment to a group of children. A man walked up and asked how the system worked, and my friend requested a piece of identification so he could show him. The man handed over his driver's license.

When the officer ran the information through the computer, the search revealed that the man was suspected of armed robbery in another city.

Let me tell you, that guy was surprised when my buddy handcuffed and arrested him.

Courtesy of Cindy Furnare

A SPEEDING "HUG"

A minister friend of mine told me this story about the time he got pulled over on his way to a revival in Nashville, Ga., back in 1979. He was staying with a church elder who lived near Valdosta, and on the night of the revival, they loaded up the car with some church folks and headed for Nashville, about 20 miles away.

When you drive into Valdosta there are no signs warning "Reduce Speed Ahead," but there's always an officer waiting to catch you if you're speeding. Now my friend had an 80-year-old reverend in the car who had warned him about the "speed trap," but since they had a baptism that night, everybody was excited to get to the revival. My friend drove right past that "City of Valdosta, Speed Limit 35 mph" sign.

Suddenly, the blue lights flashed, and my friend pulled over. The old reverend asked, "What are you doing?"

My friend said, "I think there's someone who wants to talk to me."

The old reverend crooked his neck around, saw the blue lights and said, "Now, I've been telling you he'd get you."

Well, the officer wasn't a "he" but a "she," and my friend could tell she had a sense of humor when she shined her light into the car and commented, "Sure looks like you got your hands full."

My buddy stood there in the pouring rain and gave the officer his license. She smiled, handed it back and said, "Here, take this, and drive more carefully. The good Lord is with you tonight."

My friend was so happy he gave the officer a big old hug and said, "You know, I believe you're the most beautiful thing I've seen in a long time!" The officer laughed and waved good-bye.

When my buddy climbed back in the car, the old reverend said, "I've never seen anything like that in all my life."

Courtesy of Rev. Vernon W. Harris

HARLEY, YOU SAY?

Sometimes, officers dealing with difficult situations still manage to keep a sense of humor. Here's a story I heard from a friend:

She and her husband were both officers in California. Their new baby was born prematurely, so they were awfully tired trying to work the night shift and care for their child.

Well, my friend told me that one night her husband was working on patrol when he came upon what appeared to be a traffic fatality. He was directing traffic around the scene when another officer discovered that the dead man had been shot. It looked like it would be a long night.

When the Homicide Unit finally showed up with the coroner to investigate, it was early in the morning, and, by this time, my friend's husband was exhausted. All he wanted to do was get home. But, as tired as he was, the next thing that happened still made him laugh.

As the homicide investigator bent over the body searching for some identification, he called out that he had found the victim's name.

The coroner said, "Read it to me," and he wrote down what the homicide officer read aloud: "H-A-R-L-E-Y D-A-V-I-D-S-O-N!"

Now, that's a long night!

POLICE WORK CAN BE MESSY

I heard a really "sick" story from a friend in California. In 1975, she was working the night shift as a police assistant at a department in Alameda County when an officer brought a drunk in for a breathalyzer test. It was her job to book the drunk and administer the test.

She sat the man down and showed him how the machine worked. She blew into the tube – the whole deal. That old drunk just sat there watching, she said.

When his turn came to blow into the tube, she started counting and told him to blow. He took a big, deep breath, leaned back and vomited all over her blue uniform.

The things we officers have to deal with.

BEHIND THE GRUNGE WAS A GROOM

I heard a sort of heart-warming story from friend in California who was working as an emergency services dispatcher in Santa Clara County back in 1978.

A group of officers had brought some criminals in to be booked. The place was busy, and she was just finishing up the criminal histories. The other officers had left the room when a man with a rough beard came up behind her. He had prison parole papers sticking out of the pocket of his denim shirt and he was wearing blue jeans. She thought he was a bad guy. "Can you help me out?" he said.

She was sort of nervous, and asked, "How did you get in here?"

"I came in with the rest of them," he answered.

My friend backed slowly away. "Just stay right here, buddy. You aren't going anywhere!"

"Hey, this isn't what you think," he said.

My friend replied, "You can explain it to the other guys." She picked up the phone, called the sergeant and said, "I need some help!" The sergeant sent several officers right away.

As it turns out, the man was working undercover as a burglar, and when my friend learned that, she was pretty embarrassed. The funny part is she ended up marrying him. When the local paper ran a story about their marriage, the headline read: "The Benefits of a Sting Operation!"

I guess you never know who you'll meet in this job.

HER SILENT PARTNER

A friend told me a funny story from her days as a young officer. Back in 1975, she was driving the police ambulance unit. One of the local bail bondsmen had been shot and killed, and she had to deliver his body to the hospital so the coroner could have a look.

When she stopped at an intersection, she heard a noise in the back. The body had rolled right up to the cab of the van, the sheet had come off, and that dead man was staring her right in the eye.

That shook her up so badly, she stopped the van and got out for some air. Taking one more deep breath, she climbed back in, secured the body and drove to her destination singing "Amazing Grace" the whole way there.

When the coroner asked her what took so long, she blamed it on traffic.

TAKING CARE OF BUSINESS

S ome time ago, I was asked to take a civilian along on my night shift patrol as part of a citizen's police academy project. I didn't mind since it was nice to have the company and good to let people see what police really do.

In the early morning, we got a call to investigate "suspicious noises and activity."

Well, the address was familiar since I had been called to this location before on a similar report. It was the home of an elderly woman who had developed a fairly active imagination in her old age. She was convinced there were people in her attic walls – children running back and forth disrupting her television reception.

Normally, a quick inspection and a few knocks on the walls

were enough to scare away these "delinquents" and satisfy her. I explained this to my rider who seemed surprised. She said, "You actually get these kinds of calls?"

"It's police work," I said. "This is what I'm paid to do."

Now, a second officer who was also familiar with the woman arrived too. We did a thorough inspection, banged on the walls, called those bad guys out and ordered them to leave. Unfortunately, the homeowner still believed they were in her walls. Again, we knocked and shouted and shined our lights, but it just wasn't good enough. She demanded we capture and arrest them.

Then I got an idea. I kept searching for the bad guys while the other officer walked to my cruiser and took my rider to the rear of the house. A few minutes later he called that he had captured one of the intruders.

The elderly woman and I walked back. I told the "suspect" she was under arrest, handcuffed her and announced that I was taking the culprit to jail. Now the homeowner was happy.

I put the rider in the back of my cruiser and we drove off. Down the road, I freed my "prisoner" and thanked her for her kind support of our efforts.

We had a good laugh over coffee and doughnuts at the end of my shift.

Courtesy of Barry Vance

A NAKED DESIRE

I heard a funny incident involving a friend when she was on special duty at a university. She was patrolling the campus as part of a special task force trying to solve a string of burglaries.

About 2 a.m., she heard yelling and stopped her car to listen. The sound was coming from a nearby parking lot, so she got out of her car and peeked through the bushes. What she saw was a BMW parked in the middle of the lot with a naked man dancing around it, hooting and hollering. Then he jumped back in the car and drove away.

She caught up with the streaker's car and pulled him. When she walked up to the car, the man had his pants in his lap, and his girlfriend was totally embarrassed. The officer said to the young man, "Why were you running around the parking lot naked and yelling?"

"Well, I just graduated, and I've always wanted to do that."

Unfortunately for him, there was a warrant for his arrest. So she congratulated him on his graduation and then hauled him off to jail.

Courtesy of Dana Archer

AN HONEST FACE ISN'T ENOUGH

Shortly after the Watergate Scandal and the resignation of President Nixon, I had stopped a gentleman for speeding. As soon as I told him how fast he was going, he assured me he hadn't been.

I had heard that before many times, so I asked him to have a seat in my police car, while I wrote the ticket. He immediately started repeating the phrase "I wasn't going that fast." After several times, I decided to see if I could calm him down, so I stopped writing, looked him directly in the eye, and said, "Sir, don't I look like an honest man?"

He looked back at me and in a calm voice replied, "Yes, sir, you do, but so did President Nixon."

PLEASE PASS THE CHICKEN

On a hot summer day, I had pulled over a vehicle with very dark tinted windows. Approaching the driver's side without being able to see any movement inside the car was somewhat intimidating. All of a sudden, the window started down very slowly and that made me more wary. I put my hand on my weapon, ready to respond to whatever happened.

The next thing I saw was a large plate of chicken bones coming out the window and a woman's voice saying, "Officer, if you don't mind, would you please put them bones over in the ditch? And I'm sorry. If we had known you were coming, we would have got some extra."

CANNONBALL SPECIAL

A funny thing happened to me when I was a rookie. I was on patrol about 2:30 a.m. in a rural area. The road was quiet – not much traffic.

Then, down the way, I saw a light heading toward me. I thought, "Now here's a car with a defective headlight coming my way – a chance to make a stop."

I waited until it got a little closer, then carefully aimed my radar gun. Only 38 mph? I thought, "Well, this must be a drunk driver coming from a bar somewhere." Then I watched the light slowly drift off the highway.

"He must have gone in the ditch," I decided. I hit my lights and rushed to the scene only to find a darned train heading my way.

Courtesy of Keith DeYoung

DO AS I SAY . . . .

One day my chief was lecturing a rookie officer, trying to give the young man some insight into what it was really like to be a cop.

He lectured him on professionalism, job stress and quick thinking. He went on to explain that police officers often have to make snap decisions that lawyers would debate for years. He lectured the man on being prepared to meet any challenge. He lectured him on law and procedures. He told the young man that if he always appeared to be a professional, then he would always come out on top.

The chief gave him the following pointers:

1. Always speak with authority;

2. Always stand upright with your chest out to show pride in yourself and your profession; and

3. Always wear a clean-pressed and well-maintained uniform because that would make him an officer in the public's eye.

As the Chief walked away with all the confidence he had given the young rookie, knowing he had shared the benefit of all his years of experience, I noticed the rookie looking down. He was watching the chief's fly. It had been unzipped the whole time.

Courtesy of D. J. Martin

CONFUSED MIND

Now here's a funny story a buddy of mine tells about a wanna-be bank robber he arrested once.

It seems the man planned to rob a Bank of America. He wrote a stick-up-note that read, "This is a stikkup. Put all your muny in this bag." But, while he was standing in line to hand the note to the teller, he must have worried that someone may have seen him write it, so he decided to go across the street and rob the Wells Fargo Bank.

After waiting in line at the second bank, he approached the window and handed the teller his note. Judging from the man's spelling, the teller figured he wasn't too bright, so she said politely, " I'm sorry, sir, this is a Bank of America slip. You'll either have to fill out a Wells Fargo slip or go back to the Bank of America."

Now totally confused, the man felt defeated, so he said, "Okay" and left.

The teller called police, and my buddy arrested the guy as he waited in line at the Bank of America. What a dumb crook!

Courtesy of Joe Hill

HORSING AROUND

N ow, here's a wild story that I heard from a friend who is a police officer in Alabama:

He was out on patrol one night when he received a strange radio call. Seems some fellow officers needed assistance at a location where they had, as they put it, "stopped a car with two drunks and a horse in the back."

When my buddy arrived on the scene, sure enough, there was a very old car with the back seat removed. In its place were two drunks and a pony. Seems the men had put the pony in the car and started getting drunk on their way to the farm.

Courtesy of Gamble Dick

YES, IT'S A REAL BADGE, AND IT'S MINE

Let me just tell you a story that demonstrates how dumb some crooks can really be:

A cop I know was working the midnight shift in Michigan City, Ind., and he was dispatched to a suspected robbery at a hospital pharmacy. Another unit arrived first and radioed that the suspects were trying to flee the scene. My buddy spotted the suspects pulling away slowly with their headlights off, and the chase was on.

Unfortunately, the police department's budget was tight that year, so my friend was driving what he considered to be a "junk car," and the suspects got away.

Several years later, the officer was working on an undercover operation posing as a "fence" purchasing stolen merchandise. One of the suspects he was keeping an eye on arrived at the same time every week to sell items he had stolen from local homes.

One day, after closing a deal, the suspect told my friend that he knew of a city where the cops were really dumb and their equipment was terrible. He went on to say that they were so dumb, he had once robbed a hospital pharmacy there and was able to outrun the cops. My buddy asked him where that happened, and the guy said, "Michigan City." The cop struggled to keep a straight face.

A couple of weeks later, the man was arrested for robbery, and my buddy visited him in jail. The officer showed his badge, and the man asked where he found it. "Up in Michigan City about six years ago when I was sworn in!"

To this day, the man doesn't understand or won't believe that the guy he was talking to was actually a police officer. Now, that's a dumb crook!

Courtesy of Don Siddall

WORKING LIKE A DOG

Let me share a story with you from a friend of mine in Alabama. On a Sunday afternoon my friend, a deputy at the time, was reading a summons to a young woman in the doorway of her rural home when he heard a scratching, digging sound coming from the hallway. All at once, a large bulldog ran past him like a bullet, leaped off the porch and bounded out of sight in a flash. The deputy finished reading the summons and wished the lady a good day.

As he approached his police car, it looked like someone was sitting in the front passenger seat. Getting closer, he realized he had left the door open, and his rider was the bulldog who had buzzed by him only minutes before. He wanted to get the dog out before anyone could see what had happened, but the dog warned him with a firm growl that he was happy where he was.

The deputy walked back to the house and explained the situation to the woman. Laughing, she told him the registered bulldog was often hired out for stud service. "He thinks he's going to work."

OLD HABITS, WELL, YOU KNOW . . .

Now, here's a story I heard a while back about a crook who just couldn't break the habit. He was an inmate in Walla Walla (Washington) State Penitentiary back in the days when a convict really had to work to convince a parole board to take a chance on him. The convict had to have a job, a place to stay, a squeaky clean record, and a few people in high places pulling for him. A little bit of luck didn't hurt either.

One such man was Charlie Brown. While in prison, he made all the right sounds and moves, had no disciplinary reports and had a prison counselor pulling for him.

The counselor thought old Charlie deserved a chance. Although he was doing time for armed robbery and had an extensive record, the counselor went to bat for him. He found Charlie a job and a place to stay. Charlie sang a song of repentance and remorse before the parole board, and the counselor spoke on his behalf. The board granted him his freedom.

When Charlie was released, and the prison van provided him a ride to the downtown bus station. A corrections officer bought his ticket and left him there to wait about 15 minutes for the bus, while the officer went to the courthouse to take care of business.

Now, Charlie had $100 that was just burning a hole in his pocket, so he went into the gift shop to buy some gum. A lone attendant was on duty, a young fellow who looked easily intimidated, so, I guess, the old armed robber just couldn't resist.

Charlie put his hand into his pocket to simulate a gun and said, "This is a stick-up! Hand 'er over!"

Well, the sheriff happened to wander in right about then, walked up behind Charlie and said, "I bet my gun is bigger than your gun."

To make a long story short, the judge and the district attorney just happened to be in court setting up a golf date, so Charlie was quickly arraigned. He waived his right to trial, pleaded guilty and was sentenced to 10 more years in prison. He was placed in cuffs, belly chain and leg irons and taken back to his cell, which hadn't even been cleaned out yet.

When the counselor who had fought for Charlie's freedom heard about this, he went right down to the prison to see for himself. Charlie was seated on his bunk, slumped over with his head in his hands. "What happened?" the counselor asked.

Old Charlie broke down in tears. "I tried, counselor! God knows, I tried!"

Courtesy of Joe Pierre

RECKLESS SHOPPING??

A buddy of mine told me about the time he stopped a man pushing a loaded shopping cart down the middle of a busy highway – and creating a dangerous situation. To teach him a lesson, my buddy cited him for "operating a non-motorized vehicle on a highway in a manner to create a traffic hazard."

When the case went to court, the judge wanted a description of the "non-motorized vehicle." When my buddy answered, "a shopping cart," the whole place burst into laughter.

Courtesy of David J. Ray

SEEN ANY CAT SKELETONS LATELY?

O ne night, a buddy of mine was on patrol, and as he was strolling through a residential area, twirling his baton, an elderly woman ran up to him and said, "Officer, my kitty has climbed this tree." He looked up and, sure enough, the cat was high up in that old tree. "Will you get her down?" the woman pleaded.

My buddy took a deep breath and said, "Ma'am, have you ever seen a cat skeleton hanging from a tree?"

"Of course not!" she replied.

"Well, I guess she will come down on her own then," he answered as he walked off.

Courtesy of Ted M. Arnold

FLOATING HUMOR

Awhile back, I was involved in a trial where the defense lawyer, the prosecutor and the justice of the peace were all good friends of mine, and I had caught the defendant carrying a few grams of cocaine.

The night I arrested the man, he had tried to run away by heading into a clump of bushes. I chased him down, my flashlight trailing his tracks. He disappeared for a moment, and when I caught up with him, he was treading water in a large drainage ditch. A plastic baggie of dope was floating next to his hand.

During the trial, I was being cross-examined by the defense attorney who asked if there was any possible way the baggie could have already been floating in the water before the man fell in, since the ditch was near an old garbage dump.

I answered, "No possible way."

He then asked me how deep the water was, and I told him there was no way I was going into that dirty water to find out, but I would be glad to take everyone there so they could see for themselves.

By that point, everybody was laughing. The defendant probably felt sure he was "cooked," but he got lucky, and wound up getting off with a large fine.

The justice in his parting words told the defendant, "You would have gone to jail except for all the humor provided by the bench."

I guess it goes to show that a little humor benefits everyone in the long run.

Courtesy of D. F. Rogers

HE COOKED HIS OWN GOOSE

When I worked at a precinct near a big duck pond, I knew this old sergeant who wasn't very popular. Now, I don't know who pulled this prank because it could have been any number of people, since the old sergeant tended to bend a lot of cops' feathers.

There were Canadian geese at the pond and every now and then one of them, unfortunately, would get hit by a passing car. One day, when the old sergeant finished his shift, he drove all the way home with a dead goose dragging from the back of his car. He just couldn't figure out why people who passed him were giving him dirty looks and the old middle finger sign.

We all got a good laugh out of that one.

Courtesy of Al Schulze

RIGHT CAR, WRONG DOOR

Arriving home after a busy night with the Halloween trick-or-treaters, the deputy pulled his police car close to the kitchen door to protect it from tossed eggs or other flying objects that just might fall from the sky on this night of goblins. He immediately went to bed, but it wasn't long before the ringing phone awakened him with word of a possible family dispute fueled by alcohol.

He reached for his clothes and dressed as he headed to his 1963 Chevy station wagon that had been converted into one of the sharpest police cruisers in the country. Spinner hubcaps, blue lights and whip antennas were just part of the beauty of this beast. Naturally, the back inside door and window handles had been removed the same day the protective screen had been positioned between the front and rear seats.

Hurriedly, the officer pulled the door open, and leaped in only to discover as soon as the door slammed that he had entered this prize possession of law enforcement through the wrong door.

As he sat in the back seat, he could see how securely it was built. And he knew it was going to be a long night before family members rescue him from his monster machine.

Courtesy of Alton King

ATHLETE'S FOOT ATTACK

I heard a good one from a buddy who worked for the Louisville, Ky., police department back in the 1960s – what he calls "the good old days when all police cars were two-man cars, when everyone worked shifts, and when there was no EMS."

He and his partner had just finished roll call and made it to the gas pump to fill the tank when they received a call to check on a sick person at a location quite a few miles from where they were. They started on their way with no lights or sirens.

When they arrived, they noticed three or four cars in the drive and a well-dressed woman standing in the door. My buddy, who was riding shotgun, jumped out and asked the woman if there had been a "sick call" from this address. She answered, "Yes."

"Where is the sick person?" he asked.

"Well, it's me."

"What's wrong with you Ma'am?"

"I have athlete's foot real bad," she answered.

Now, at this point, the officer in the car started laughing while my buddy was in shock. He asked her if she could drive and she said she could, so he advised her to climb into one of the cars and take herself to the hospital. He turned and walked away not knowing whether to laugh or cry.

Courtesy of James H. Simon

BAD-D-D-D-D VEHICLE

A friend of mine was running radar on Georgia 411 south one night when he happened to check a Chevy that was traveling north 25 mph over the speed limit.

He said the driver must have seen his cruiser crossing the median, because when the officer reached the halfway point, the driver was already parked on the side of the road and out of the car. As the officer approached, the driver removed his belt and began whipping his car, screaming, "Bad car! Bad car!"

My buddy sat there until he felt the offending vehicle had been punished enough. He approached the driver, cautioned him about owning a car he could not control, got back in his cruiser and drove off – without giving the man a ticket.

NOT IN MY CELL, YOU DON'T

I heard this funny story from a man arrested for reckless driving in a very small town. Since there was no room for him in its jail, the jailer and the officer decided to lock him in the bathroom until a transport vehicle could take him to a nearby town. "Now, this is your cell," they told him.

Once inside, the prisoner took a seat on the commode. In that position, he realized the door locked from the inside, meaning the jailer and the officer couldn't lock him in, but he could lock them out. And he did just that.

A little while later, the doorknob rattled and a deep voice boomed, "Boy, you'd better open this door. I need to use the bathroom bad."

Not worrying much about the outcome, the man replied, "Not in my cell, you don't!"

Courtesy of James in Kentucky

DYING, COMING AND GOING

Here's one traffic stop I'll never forget even though some days everybody you stop for speeding is going to or coming from a funeral.

I stopped this elderly couple for speeding, and the gentleman was out of the car before I could put my hat on and dismount. As we met halfway, he began, "You just don't understand, officer. I'm coming from a funeral down in Alabama." I told him I was sorry to hear about the death in his family.

He went on to say that while the family was at Uncle Joe's grave site, someone delivered the message that Aunt Josey had passed away in Michigan, and he and his wife were on their way to that funeral. I instructed him to have a seat in my cruiser.

I walked up to his car and bent down to speak to his wife. "Ma'am, I am really sorry to hear about so many deaths in your family."

"Who died?" she asked. I repeated what her husband had said, and she replied, "Did Joe tell you that? He's getting to where he lies all the time."

FULL OF THE HOLIDAY SPIRIT

As a newly assigned trooper at a rural state police post, I was working a lot of hours during the holiday season, and Christmas night a sheriff's deputy and I were patrolling the county. We were headed for a cup of coffee when we spotted a vehicle parked on the side of the road. The headlights were off and the driver's door was open.

I dismounted my cruiser, cautiously approached to check the situation and saw a man slumped over the steering wheel. It turned out to be a good-size drunk driver – the man weighed close to 300 pounds – and he was passed out. I pulled, pushed and tugged, but could not roust him from sleep or get him out of the vehicle. Even with the deputy's help, we had no luck.

I stepped back to evaluate the situation and, it being Christmas and all, to just let him be. As we drove off, I wished him a Merry Christmas!

WARNING: TOW TRUCK A'COMIN'

Everyone should have an uncle like I had – a gentleman who loved life and everything about it. One autumn day while I was sitting on the Western Kentucky Parkway in front or behind (depended on which way you were traveling) a large bush in the median, here comes my uncle, Willard Stith, driving a new large white van-type bread truck and pulling another just like it. He had picked them up in Michigan and was delivering them to Texas.

Spotting me, he pulled over in the emergency lane, and got in my car. Just as he closed the door, a speeder went by at better than 90 mph. I told him to hang on, and away we went down the road about a mile before the violator pulled over.

After arresting the driver for being intoxicated, I called for a wrecker to tow his car. After waiting about 30 minutes, I got concerned and called the dispatcher who advised me the truck had been sent 30 minutes ago.

About that time I looked in my rear view mirror and saw a little red tow truck pulling two new, large white vans that looked just like the ones my uncle had left on the side of the road.

I said Willard loved life because he laughed until the bread trucks were back into his hands, and down the road to Texas he went, still laughing.

WATCH FOR FLASHING LIGHTS

A friend of mine told me about an embarrassing moment he had with a state trooper. He was driving down a rural highway one night when every car that passed him blinked their lights on and off. It happened so many times he actually stopped his car and got out to see what was wrong. What were all these folks were trying to tell him? His lights seemed to be working okay, so he climbed back in and continued on his way. But it kept happening! Every car that passed flashed its lights.

Just then, he noticed a state trooper sitting on the side of the road, so he pulled up, got out and asked the trooper to inspect his vehicle. "Why?" the trooper asked.

"Well, officer, every darned car that passes me, flashes its lights like something's wrong."

The trooper laughed and said, "Maybe that's cause I'm here, friend!"

Man, did my buddy feel dumb.

Courtesy of Rick Chinn

JUST ONE LITTLE JOY RIDE

N ow, motorist assistance is an important part of police work, especially in rural areas. One night on patrol, I spotted a 1957 pickup sitting on the side of the road with the hood open. I stopped to find a young woman wrestling with the motor, trying to get the shift-lever unstuck. Well, it just so happened that I'd had the same problem with my own truck, so I insisted on giving it a try.

After crawling under the hood and down around the shift-lever, I heard my cruiser pull off. I jumped up and watched the woman driving away. Since I had fixed her pickup, I climbed into it and took off in pursuit.

When I finally caught up to her, she had parked the cruiser and was standing right there beside it. "Now don't get excited," she said. "I've always wanted to drive a police cruiser, and I knew if I asked, you'd have said no."

What can you do?

Courtesy of Don Young

ANYBODY GET THE PLATE NUMBER OF THAT BED?

There was a late-night crash involving a drunk driver who drove off the road, through the side of a house and into the bedroom of a sleeping couple. I was only a few blocks away when I got the call over the radio. Arriving at the scene, I found the drunk arguing with the young couple.

The driver told me he left the road because another car passed him and forced him off the roadway while its two occupants were asleep on top of the car. Not only was he upset with the couple, but he was unhappy with me because I wouldn't give them a ticket for causing the crash.

I tried to explain to him why I couldn't give them a ticket: First of all, the bed they were on wasn't a registered motor vehicle, so the traffic laws didn't apply to it, and, secondly, there is no law against sleeping on a bed while traveling down a public highway.

POP, GOES THE SUNROOF

This story comes from a brother Kentucky State Police officer who was patrolling the Western Kentucky Parkway.

He pulled over a Lincoln Continental for speeding, and as he talked with the driver, he realized there were five passengers in the front seat and six in the back. He wrote the driver a speeding ticket, and added that before she could move the car, she would have to rearrange passengers because five in the front seat was hazardous.

The officer was headed back to his cruiser when he heard the Lincoln's sunroof open, and as the car pulled away, three heads popped out. He guessed those three were standing between the front and back seats.

Courtesy of B. Stafford

THANKS, BUT NO THANKS

One time when I was on patrol, I found a man who appeared to be intoxicated walking along the road. I thought I'd be kind and offer him a ride home, since I was in a good mood that night. I stopped, put him in the back of my cruiser and drove on toward his destination.

A little way down the road, a dog ran out in front of me, so I hit the brakes. I turned my head around just in time to see my passenger's face pressed right up against the separating cage.

When I dropped him off, the old boy said, "Thanks for the ride, officer, but I think I'd rather have walked."

Courtesy of Joe Scudder

CHOICES, CHOICES AND MORE CHOICES

S itting in a little restaurant across from the local bank with the town's police chief, I wondered what he would do if he saw a robber coming out of the bank with a bag in his hands. So I asked him, and here was his reply:

"Well, Leo, I have often thought of that, and it might be one of the major decisions of my career. If I got to chasing him and was almost where I could catch him, I have wondered what I would do. What if he had all my bank notes in that bag? Would I really want to catch him and return them to the bank? Well, I got to thinking, he couldn't carry all my loan notes anyway."

Then he turned to me and said, "You're buying lunch today."

Courtesy of Chief Austin Wooden

WHO CUT DOWN THE CHERRY TREE?

T he wife of a friend told me this funny tale the other day. It seems, she and her husband, a Kentucky State trooper, had a strange encounter with several men from Louisville, Ky., who were doing some work on the local courthouse, and camping at night near Cumberland Lake. One night the men left camp to get food and drinks, and on their way back, they got lost.

They showed up at my friends' house asking for directions to their camp. Two of the men were drunk as all get-out, but a third man, the camp cook, was sober and quite upset. Seems they had been driving down every side road they saw trying to find their camp. A five-foot cherry tree was caught in the bumper, and the car was covered with dents. They had hit the walls on both sides of Wolf Creek Dam

The trooper identified himself, and told the drunks he would have to take them to jail. They were pretty upset, but they went along. The cook slept right out in the couple's front yard.

The next morning, the two went before a judge and paid a fine. When they came back to the house with her husband and saw their car, they couldn't believe their eyes. The owner of the car shouted, "My wife will kill me when she sees this!"

Courtesy of Mrs. Maxine Butler

YOU TALK TOO MUCH

Here's a funny story from a friend in Ohio:

He was working at an Army camp down in Florida back in 1940, and he was one of the few soldiers who had a car. One weekend, he took a trip to Atlanta to see his brother. On his way back, he was stopped by a friendly patrolman who gave him a warning for driving too fast and passing on a hill with a double yellow line.

When the officer told him to go on his way and be careful, my buddy was so happy about not getting a ticket, he said, "Thanks, officer. I thought you were stopping me because my tags were expired." The officer walked to the back of his car to have a look, smiled and wrote him a ticket.

When my friend told his wife, her reply was: "You talk too much!"

Courtesy of Henry L. Combs

WHERE IS THAT LICENSE WHEN YOU NEED IT

Let me tell you about the time I was working the graveyard shift: It was about 2 a.m. when I saw a car weaving down the road, and signaled for it to stop. I asked the driver for his license and vehicle registration. He had neither.

Naturally suspicious, I questioned him further: "You mean you don't have your license with you or it's been revoked?"

The man sort of hesitated, then replied: "This is the first time in my life I've ever needed one."

Courtesy of P. J. Lawton

WHAT A BIG MOUTH

One summer day I received a radio transmission from headquarters to head to a doctor's office in my hometown. When I got there, I could hear a young man screaming at the top of his lungs up on the second floor. He was using all kinds of profanity and throwing things around. When I reached the top of the stairs, I was just in time to watch him throw a chair across the room.

I asked him what the problem was, and he said the doctor would not give him pills. Turns out he had asked the doctor for a prescription, and the doctor flat out refused.

He was yelling and cursing as he pushed magazines off a table and kicked them around the floor. Then he said he was going to burn down the medical plaza.

I told him if he didn't calm down he was going to jail. At this point, he asked if he could smoke some pot. "That's what I always do to keep from burning down a building. Pot calms me down."

I couldn't believe the question. But then, the man pulled

out a pipe and a bag full of grassy material. "What the hell's that?" I asked.

"Pot," he responded.

"No way!" I said, grabbing the bag from his hand. Sure enough, it was marijuana, so I pulled out the cuffs.

I took him to headquarters and while he was being booked, he asked again if he could smoke some pot. I said, "Sorry, pal, but I got it all."

"Not all of it," he said. "I got more in my car."

Well, I finally talked him into telling me where his car was, and officers found a quarter-pound of marijuana-hash mix hidden in it. I informed the young man that he was in a lot more trouble, adding, "Tough break. I do have it all now!"

"No sh*#! Don't you think I have more?" he countered.

I challenged him: "I know you don't have anymore."

"I got lots more at my house, you moron!"

I told him I didn't believe that and dared him to let me search for it. The fool took the dare and signed the consent form. When the search team returned, they had two more pounds of marijuana.

The craziest part of this crazy story is that when the case went to court, the young man claimed he had been framed and knew nothing about any of the illegal drugs we had in our possession.

Courtesy of William A. Connell

NEVER DRIVE UNDRESSED

"**B**eing a single parent is never easy. You have to make ends meet by taking on several jobs and working until you can hardly stay awake. When this incident happened, I was working a day job from 8-5 and leaving there to go to my evening job, at a restaurant. The food was very good, and one of the perks of the job was a free supper, which lowered the grocery bill. The buffet was very good on this particular evening, so I really filled up.

"Getting off work late was a normal thing for me as I always liked to stay until the last tip was laid on the table. It was 3 a.m. when I left the restaurant. After a long day and a lot of food, I decided to get comfortable for the long ride home. We lived 40 miles from the city where I worked. So I took off the panty hose I had been wearing for the last 17 hours and unzipped my skirt, since I had so much good food that evening.

"I drove about 20 miles south down the interstate and was just between the next to the last and the last exit before getting off the freeway toward home. All of a sudden the wind blew and I turned around quickly to see what all the commotion was about. I was about half-asleep, and when I turned my head to the left, my hand automatically turned with it and into median I went. It turned out the louvers on the back of my Datsun 200SX had blown off into the highway.

"At this point I didn't know what to do. I was stuck in the muddy median with no hope of driving out on my own. So I blinked my headlights on and off, on and off until a kind state trooper pulled over to assist me.

"I was sitting in the car and he asked me to get out. He wanted to test me to make sure that I wasn't drinking. I had forgotten all about how comfortable I had gotten and proceeded to get out of the car. Well, you know some women don't wear panties and pantyhose too, and I'm one of those. When I got out of the car, my unzipped skirt fell completely down to my ankles, and, much to the officer's surprise, he saw the moon on a very cloudy night (if you know what I mean).

"He quickly turned his head, and asked, "Ma'am, have you been drinking this evening?"

I replied, "No, just working."

"What type of work do you do or should I ask?" he responded, and I told him.

"He was very nice, and took me to the next exit where I called my cousin for help. I guess the lesson learned here is 'Never get caught with your hose down.'"

SCARED STIFF AS A STATUE

A friend of mine in the military was transferred from Niagara Falls, N.Y., to Fort Knox, Ky. Since he had worked in law enforcement for more than 25 years, when he got to Radcliff he was interviewed by the police chief for a part-time position on the force and was hired.

For two weeks, he rode with a training officer to learn the ropes. Seems the chief also wanted to know how he would react to certain situations. Eventually, he was issued his own patrol car.

One night, he discovered an open window at an old church. Coming from New York, he was accustomed to going into dangerous situations alone, but the local policy was to always call for backup, so he radioed for assistance. The officer who had trained him came, and the two entered the church – my buddy through the front and the other officer through the rear.

Well, a few minutes later, my buddy heard his backup shout, "Keep your hands up and don't move!" My buddy came running when the officer added, "C'mon, I got him covered!"

The officer definitely had the suspect "covered," but when

the lights were turned on his weapon was pointed at a statue of the Virgin Mary. Now, if you've ever been in a Catholic church, you know the Holy Mother stands with her hands out-stretched. My buddy said he tried not to laugh as the officer lowered his weapon, embarrassed.

When my friend made out his report he wrote, "Officer was about to shoot the Blessed Mother."

Courtesy of Joseph M. Howard

ASSIST BY THE ARRESTEE

I know a guy who got some unexpected help from the suspect he was pursuing. My buddy was training a rookie in an unfamiliar section of West Philadelphia when a call came in: "Officer needs assistance!" Neither my friend nor the rookie knew their location, so they hurriedly read the map, searching for their whereabouts.

Just then, a stroke of luck! The suspect ran past their cruiser. My buddy jumped out and started a pursuit. He chased the guy for 10 blocks until he could run no longer. Out of breath and exhausted, he stopped, regained his balance and hurled his nightstick at the suspect. It struck the man on the back, but the blow didn't do much to slow him down.

The chase began again, but frustrated and tired, my buddy stopped. He hunched over, hands on his knees, and breathing hard. He looked up to see the suspect was bent over in the same position about 10 houses ahead of him.

Then, a call requesting the officer's location came over the portable radio. He couldn't find a street sign anywhere, so he answered, "I don't know."

The suspect yelled, "59th and Ogden!" My friend reported his location.

The suspect yelled, "You ready to continue the chase?" The officer shouted, "Yes!" And the two darted off.

A little way down the road, cruisers arrived to give the officer a hand and the suspect was arrested.

After being taken into custody, suspect offered to lead my buddy back to the location where he had lost his nightstick. Can you believe that?

Courtesy of Bob Ralston

A NOT-SO-TASTY SURPRISE

Now talk about something sick: Here's a story from a friend out in Seattle who received a call to report to a motor home park. When he got there, he found a man curled into a ball next to a puddle of raw sewage. He was as ill as you could ever imagine.

My friend asked what was wrong. The man said he'd been trying to steal gasoline, and had plugged his hose into the sewage tank by mistake. When he tried to siphon the gasoline, he wound up with a mouthful of sewage instead!

The owner of the motor home was not upset. In fact, he told my friend it was the best laugh he ever had.

Courtesy of Cindy Furnare

INTERSTATE-USE ONLY

One time, I was dispatched to a reported theft of a car battery. When I arrived, there sat an old Mercury Comet in the front yard of the house, and the owner was standing beside it. He was very upset and requested the FBI be notified, fingerprints be taken and an "APB" be put out on the stolen battery.

Well, I dusted for prints, but found none, since the underside of the hood was pretty dirty. The crazy thing was the thief had left a new battery in place of the old one.

When I interviewed the man, I learned he didn't know the brand of the missing battery and couldn't describe it any better than it was black with red buttons on the top. He had no insurance to cover the loss. I told him I would file a report, but there wasn't much of a chance the missing battery would be found.

Then I asked him if the battery that had been left in his car worked. He said it had worked just fine before I arrived. So I asked him why he didn't just use it?

He looked at me as if I were crazy, and asked if I could read. Pecking the battery with his finger, he asked, "What does it say right here on top of this battery?"

I said, "Interstate."

"You see there, trooper, there's no way I can use this battery. I never go any farther than Manchester!"

Courtesy of Carl Elliott

A BLUE AND WHITE WAVE

Here's a good story from a true University of Kentucky fan: About three years ago, my friend was driving on the Western Kentucky Parkway in his white 1990 Oldsmobile, which he said makes all his UK stickers look real good! He said some people think he works for the university since his car is covered in so much blue and white. He claims that one time a man at the Falls of the Rough lodge was so sure my friend was C. M. Newton, he asked for an autograph.

Anyway, he was driving his car with two large UK magnetic logos attached to the doors. About 10 miles out of Elizabethtown, Ky., he noticed a black car with a whip antenna fast approaching from the rear. He then looked at his speedometer and realized it was too late to slow down. He was going to get a ticket.

The car pulled right up beside him, and the officer inside gave him a smile and a big thumbs-up sign!

I guess it pays to love the blue and white.

Courtesy of Rev. Vernon W. Harris

TO OPEN DOOR, TURN HANDLE

I remember a time when the SWAT unit was summoned to deal with a man who had barricaded himself in a room.

A SWAT team officer I knew was given the job of penetrating the room. He took position in front of the big door and began kicking to break it down. It was solid oak, and he kicked and kicked but only succeeded in knocking a wide crack in the center.

At that point, his partner reached up, turned the handle and opened the door. Boy, did my pal feel foolish!

Courtesy of Don Siddall

ASK AND YE SHALL RECEIVE

I had just cleared the office one spring day, and first on my mind was making sure there were no disabled cars on my beat. I was about halfway through my check and talking to "The Boss." I asked Him to send me someone who needed and was ready to receive His word. That was about 5:15 p.m. I traveled to the end of my beat, made a u-turn and headed for the boundary at the other end, which was the city limits of Yucca Valley. I finished checking my whole beat in another five minutes.

As I passed the Yucca Valley city limits, approximately 5:20 p.m., I noticed a vehicle traveling in the opposite direction with one of its low-beam headlights out. Usually, I don't get excited about burned-out headlights unless it's toward the end of my shift, and I was skunked on speeding or seatbelt tickets. This evening, He told me to worry about this car with the burned-out headlight, so I made a u-turn and stopped it right at the intersection, which was the city boundary.

The driver was wearing black leather gloves (my first hint something wasn't right), and I asked him to step out. As he did, he turned his back to me as if to say, "OK, I know you're going to check me for weapons, so go ahead." I patted him down and I asked him if he had any weapons. He didn't.

As I talked to him, trying to establish his identity and the ownership of the car, it was apparent he was not telling the truth about who he was and why he had the car. I determined he was lying, arrested him for giving false information and put him in my cruiser.

Then I went back to the stopped car to find its registration. What I found was the ignition had been punched, and the brand new screwdriver on the seat had grease on its tip. There was also a binder on the front seat that belonged to a waitress who worked at a local restaurant.

With more investigation, I learned the man had stolen this car from the restaurant's parking lot five minutes before I stopped him, putting the theft just about the same time I was asking the Lord for someone to bring His word to, which I obligingly did, as I drove my prisoner to jail for auto theft. He was very receptive and appeared to listen closely. Ask and ye shall receive!

JUST FOLLOWING THE SIGNS

Quite a while back, I was sitting on the side of the highway waiting to catch speeding motorists when I saw a car puttering along at 22 mph. This is just as dangerous as speeding, so I turned on my lights and pulled the driver over.

When I got to the car, I saw five elderly ladies – two in the front and three in the back – sitting there wide-eyed and white as ghosts. The driver said, "Officer, I don't understand. I was doing exactly the speed limit. What seems to be the problem?"

"Ma'am, you were going much slower than the speed limit, and that's very dangerous too."

"No sir, officer," she answered firmly. "I was doing the speed limit exactly – 22 miles per hour."

There she sat, confident and proud, as I tried not to laugh. "Ma'am, this is Route 22. That's not the speed limit."

She was embarrassed, and said, "I'm so sorry."

The passengers seemed terribly shaken, and since they hadn't muttered a peep the whole time, I asked the driver, "Are you sure everything is okay, Ma'am?"

Looking back at her riders, she said, "Oh, they'll be fine in a minute, officer. We just got off Route 119."

NO IDEA AT ALL

When a buddy of mine was a rookie trooper, he responded to an accident out in Clay County in eastern Kentucky on a one-lane gravel road.

When he got there, the two vehicles were all twisted together – paint, lights and fenders – off the road, and the drivers were standing beside them.

The officer approached one of the drivers, a man who looked to be about 75 years old, and asked for his license. The man replied, "Naw, trooper, I ain't got no license, but you know a feller needs one nowadays."

Then the trooper asked if he had any I.D. The man answered, "'Bout what, officer?"

Courtesy of Dave Norris

IT'S GOT TO BE THE SHOES

Let me tell you about the night a bunch of us were dispatched to a home where a burglary was in progress.

As we pulled up, we spotted a suspect running away, and the homeowner shouted, "There he goes!" and we started after him.

He ran. He jumped fences. He crawled on the ground. But even though that darn fool did everything to get away, it was easy for us to catch him, since his shoes were equipped with red flashing lights.

Courtesy of Mike Pittman

SPEAKING OF NATURAL GAS

Now, here's a funny story a friend tells on himself. He was driving on U.S. 460 east of Frankfort, Ky., heading toward Georgetown when he decided to speed up so he could make it there a little quicker. Just as he pressed on the accelerator, lunch caught up with him and he expelled gas.

Then he noticed the blue lights in his rear view mirror, so he stopped. The state trooper walked up just as my friend rolled down his window. The first thing the officer said was "Peeeewwwww!" as he cringed and held his nose. "May I see your license please?" the officer asked. Then waving his arms, he stepped back, and said, "Man, that's awful!"

My buddy just sat there embarrassed while the officer walked away, shouting back, "Go on! I can't take it! Just drive slower!"

Courtesy of George Harper

POSITIVE ATTITUDE, POSITIVE DAY

I love a new day. Getting up early is a habit I've come to really enjoy. The morning air is crisp, the birds seem to sing louder, and the aroma of hot coffee alerts the senses that this day is going to be my day. What a way to get started! Yes, there truly is a God in heaven, and I believe His special touch is all over each new day.

The alarm clock went off at 6 a.m. that Tuesday morning in Goshen, Ky. I rushed to shower, dress quickly, and head into work early. A typical morning, actually. Yes, today was going to be my day. "Positive Attitude, Positive Day." That was the "motto" as I drove out of our subdivision with a purpose and a plan.

We live perhaps three-quarters of a mile from the main highway, and the road is a bit narrow, so the speed limit is 25 mph. Now I know this very well. We moved into this wonderful neighborhood almost one year ago, so 25 mph is not a surprise. However, it is an obstacle to remember. So I proceeded toward the main highway enjoying the beautiful morning, daydreaming as I floated over the rolling blacktop road, and thinking of the day ahead, "Positive Attitude, Positive Day." That was my motto, remember.

I topped that last hill and, oh my goodness, what is that? It's a policeman. Immediately I knew, (don't we always know?), I was busted. I thought to myself, oh please, maybe, just perhaps, he doesn't have his radar on. No, that didn't work either. I could see through the back glass of the police car as I topped the hill, and the radar gun light popped on "red." Not a pinkish or a pale shade, but a bright fire-engine red. I was caught fair and square.

So I pulled the van over to the side of the road very quickly, and awaited my fate. Oh man, I thought, how could I be so dumb. I do not need a ticket right now. This is just terrible! Aggravating as can be. My day is ruined. Positive Attitude, Positive What? What motto?

Well, here is where the fun begins. You see, I am convinced the Lord puts us in these little situations from time to time just to keep us honest. I watched the officer get out of his patrol car, adjust his hat and gun, and begin his march to my window. "Good morning, sir," he said. "I believe you were speeding." Reluctantly, I agreed. "Yes, sir, I was. You are correct."

"May I see your license and insurance verification?" he asked. As I handed the officer what he had requested, I decided this was one of those tests the Lord gives us. The first was getting pulled over at 6:30 a.m. and remaining somewhat calm.

Here comes the second test: "Mr. Brown, is this your correct address? Dover Cove?"

"No. We moved recently into this new subdivision."

"Mr. Brown, you have fifteen days to change your address on your license after moving. When did you move, Mr. Brown," the officer asked.

Here is test number three: Should I tell a lie or . . . Ohhh ahhh uhmmm . . . "Well, it's been almost a year, sir," I replied. So I guess I passed that test too.

"Well, Mr. Brown, I need to write you a citation. I will be right back."

Have you ever noticed how long it takes a bad experience to be over? It had been perhaps 10 minutes since the radar zapped me, but it felt like three hours. So I looked around and tried to enjoy what was left of my new day, which had been ruined in a matter of minutes.

Finally, I watched the officer step from his patrol car, adjust his hat and gun, just like before, and march up to my car. I expected the worst, so as I made eye contact, I listened intently to hear the verdict.

"Mr. Brown, I really thank you for your cooperation this morning. I have written you a warning citation, sir," the officer said.

YES! YES! YES, I thought to myself. Give me a high-five. Oh yeah! "Mr. Brown, please drive carefully in the future. Always watch your speed, sir. And, by the way, because you are wearing your seat belt this morning, sir, here is a coupon for a free pizza. Drive safely, sir, and enjoy," he said as he walked away.

How do you like that? I spend what seemed like an eternity worrying, and expecting points on my driving record, a reduction in my bank account funds, and generally a "rain-on-my-parade" attitude-buster for the day, and ended up with a warning citation and a free pizza to boot. How can you beat that?

Many of my friends have since told me they are going to get pulled over just to get the free pizza for dinner. I don't want to do that again, without a doubt. However, I think we can learn two things from this little story: First, I love a "new day," and, second, God's special touch is all around us each and every new day – even if He sometimes wears a policeman's uniform and delivers pizza at 6:30 a.m.

Courtesy of Ken Brown

CPSIA information can be obtained
at www.ICGtesting.com
Printed in the USA
BVHW040300101019
560742BV00008B/79/P